MURDERGRAM
●●●●●●●

PART 2

D1559444

MURDERGRAM

PART 2

Murdergram 2. Copyright © 2015 by Melodrama Publishing. All rights reserved. No part of this book may be used or reproduced in any manner whatsoever without written permission except in the case of brief quotations embodied in critical articles or reviews. For information, address Melodrama Publishing, P.O. Box 522, Bellport, NY 11713.

www.melodramapublishing.com

Library of Congress Control Number: 2015912543
ISBN-13: 978-1620780749

First Edition: January 2016
Mass Market Edition: January 2017

Editor: Brian Sandy

Printed in Canada

ALSO BY NISA SANTIAGO

PROLOGUE

●●

The house was a horrific crime scene. Body upon body was slaughtered in what appeared to be a drug related massacre. The room was blanketed with just fewer than twenty innocent lives that were snuffed out in such a heinous act. Police radioed in for a half-dozen coroner vans, as it appeared there was no proof of life. One detective had to compose himself as he happened upon the body of the first slain child.

The next-door neighbor had reported the crime. He said he had seen a few individuals looking like stick-up kids in dark clothing lurking around the building, like they were up to no good. He said he knew someone was going to get robbed when he saw the same guys rough-handling the boyfriend, Hugo, and pushing their way inside the apartment.

"What time was that?" the detective asked.

"Yo, that was like"—He looked over his shoulder to see if anyone saw him snitching to the police—"It was like, five o' clock."

"Excuse me, did you say five?"

"Yeah, I had just finished watchin' *Judge Judy* and was on my way to my girl's crib."

"But the nine-one-one call didn't come through until six thirty."

The neighbor looked at the detective like, *And?*

"You mean you saw a robbery in progress that led to seventeen homicides, and you waited over an hour to call for help?" The detective didn't allow the witness to answer, hitting him with a two-piece—a hard left to his jaw and a quick right to the abdomen—before his partner pulled him off.

Everyone's nerves were frayed. Seeing so many dead, and the manner in which they met their fate, had the most hardened detective on high alert.

"I'ma sue ya ass!" the witness screamed, holding his chin. "The city's gonna pay up. You fucked up now! Yeah, you fucked up now! I'ma have your badge, bitch!"

"Get the fuck outta here!" another detective yelled, backing him down.

It was a tense situation going on for all involved. The building was crawling with police officers, detectives, and naturally the captain showed up on the scene because this case was that huge. Channels 7 and 4, and Fox news cameras were all parked outside to get an exclusive from friends, neighbors, and any bystander willing to give any detail about the incident.

Out of all the elderly, college students, or working-class residents, the news stations couldn't find one individual without missing teeth, a headscarf wrapped around unruly hair, or who was fluent in anything but ebonics, making the information hard to follow.

As the coroners began placing bodies in the body bags to place on the gurneys for autopsies, a loud yelp came from one of the workers. She had rolled one of the bodies into the body bag, and as she was zipping it up, the corpse inhaled deeply, startling her.

"We've got a sign of life!" she called out. "Get an ambulance out here now!"

•••

It felt like an explosion went off in her head. It was like someone had turned on the lights, which was a switch to full-blown pain. Every part of her body was in agony as a team of doctors and nurses poked and prodded.

A soft-spoken head surgeon shined a flashlight in her eyes, testing her reflexes. "Do you know your name?"

She took several seconds before she responded. "Cristal . . . my name . . . it's Cristal."

ONE

●●●●●●●●●●●●●●●●●●●●●●●●●●●●●●●●●

I t was a sweltering July evening, and hundreds of people were lined up around the block to meet the renowned author Melissa Chin at Standard Books, an eclectic, independent bookstore on the Lower East Side of Manhattan. A variety of fans—young and old, foreign and provincial—yearned to have a few words and a photo op with the gifted writer. They felt fortunate that she was in town. She was an intriguing writer; her stories jumped out of the pages and captivated her readers.

The book signing had been publicized throughout the tri-state area on radio stations and social media, and the fact that Melissa Chin had had a few guest spots on a national reality show helped to launch her new book, *Killer Dolls*. It was already on *The New York Times* Best Sellers list, was flying off the shelves everywhere, and her downloads on Amazon.com were unprecedented. It was the author's third book in less than two years, with every story being more engrossing and thrilling than the next. The murders in the book were well orchestrated, and the readers could feel the characters' untimely demises as if they were the victims.

Melissa basked in the spotlight as her handlers hovered around, warding off enthusiastic fans. She sat there behind the folding table, dozens of books piled in front of her like some kind of literary partition. She smiled, autographing book after book, and snapped pictures with a few fans.

Melissa was a stuck-up bitch, but she knew how to play nice. She had recently cut her long, soft hair into an edgy style made popular by Rihanna—shaved low on one side and long on the other. Her bright pink Candy Yum-Yum MAC lipstick accented her pink form-fitting Fendi romper. Her pale Puerto Rican skin had a subtle tan, and her gold bangles sparkled in the summer sun. Melissa wanted the moment to last forever. She was made to do this—to be famous, sitting at the table with hundreds of her books selling fast, chatting, signing copies, and taking selfies with her readers.

The cameras snapped away, flooding the room with quick flashes like a disco ball. It felt like a party. She felt high, with the attention and spotlight all on her.

As everyone in the bookstore grasped for the author's attention, snapping pictures of her from every angle, one person stood off to the side from it all, lurking.

Unbeknownst to everyone in the room, this person was the real Melissa Chin. Draped in oversized goggle shades, a fedora hat, and unassuming garb, she played her position, amused. Hiring the wannabe actress/model was a great business decision.

The young woman pretending to be Melissa Chin was really Daisy McLeod—originally from a small town in Idaho, a one-traffic-light kind of town nestled away in Middle America like summer shorts in the closet during winter.

Daisy looked immensely different now than when the twenty-five-year-old author had first found her. She had been a loner with purple-and-pink hair who listened to heavy metal and worshiped the devil. She had been a punk and a high-school dropout.

Now, she wore six-inch Louboutin heels and designer gear, and her hair was styled trendily in its original dark brown color. She was making a killing with the appearance fees she was charging Melissa, and she also had a side hustle Melissa didn't know about. She would charge $100 dollars for signed copies and $50 for photo ops, and had started charging local club promoters $2,500 per appearance. She was milking her masquerade as Melissa Chin for everything it was worth, and the money she made went to breast implants, booty-plumping injections, drugs, and having a good time.

Daisy McLeod was no longer recognizable to anyone from her past—not even to her own mother. Mrs. McLeod could have easily bypassed her own daughter in the streets and not said a single word to her.

Four hours later, the crowd in the bookstore began to dissipate.

Daisy finally sauntered over to her boss with a hard stare. "You know I'm the shit," she said. "Who can do this better than me?"

Melissa remained expressionless, looking at her protégée evenly. Their relationship was transitioning.

Daisy walked around the bookstore red-carpet style, as if walking a runway for Givenchy. She was getting all the spotlight and media attention only because of the books Melissa wrote and feared that her celebrity status and fifteen minutes of fame would vanish the moment Melissa stopped writing books. Without her, she would once again become a lost and confused no-talent, small-time girl from Idaho.

Daisy had sat down numerous times and tried to write a book herself, to piggyback on Melissa Chin's success, but there was one hiccup—she couldn't write. She didn't have the patience or the knowledge, and her creative skills were limited to spray-painting graffiti signs back in the day. She thought it would be easy to write a book, but once she realized it actually took talent, her resentment toward Melissa began to fester.

"I want two thousand per appearance from now on, a driver to pick me up and drop me off to all book signings, and I want a thousand per radio or media event I show up to, and some clothing allowance for each book signing," she said gruffly.

Melissa remained calm. She looked at the sassy nineteen-year-old bitch and saw a glimmer of her former self.

The current arrangement between them was $150 per appearance, and her publicist usually set up ten to fifteen book signings per title. The new proposal would cost

Melissa a minimum of $30,000, not including car service and clothing allowance.

"Let's be reasonable," she said to Daisy.

"This is reasonable," Daisy spat back. "Without me, you wouldn't have this. And if I decide to talk, you know, tell the public the real deal, can you imagine the ruckus that would stir up?"

Melissa's cold stare was hidden behind her dark shades. Daisy had forgotten who was the boss and ignored the golden rule—never bite the hand that feeds you.

"Either I get paid more, or I'll talk. I think you have more to lose than me. It was my face that launched a million book sales. You think your scarred face could make this happen? You need me. Don't forget that. You wouldn't be able to handle the spotlight like I can," Daisy said, hands on her hips, thinking she was in control of it all.

Melissa exhaled loudly. "Okay, we'll talk."

Daisy smiled. "I know we will." She pivoted on her expensive heels and strutted out of the bookstore like she was the best thing since Spanx.

Melissa kept her cold eyes on the young small-town girl. Daisy no idea what she'd just created for herself. Although Melissa had agreed to have a talk with Daisy to renegotiate her terms, there would be no negotiating. Daisy was only a pawn that she'd put into the game, and now that pawn needed to be put down. The Melissa Chin the world knew would have to take a nap—a permanent one.

TWO

●●●●●●●●●●●●●●●●●●●●●●●●●●●●●●●●●●●●●●

Clutching a bouquet of flowers, Sharon Green stepped out of her white Fiat 500L under the bright, hot sun and took a deep breath. The smell of freshly mown grass and flowers infiltrated her nostrils. She looked at the sprawling cemetery before her and heaved a heavy, emotional sigh. She headed toward the entrance and walked through the rusty gate leading into the path of graves spread out in every direction, the white and gray polished-granite tombstones reflecting the sunlight. Very few of the graves were cared for. It seemed like once you were dead, you were forgotten.

She walked evenly to Pike's grave and knelt before his headstone. She missed him greatly and thought about him every single day. His death was uncalled for and still unsolved. She removed the dead flowers she'd left from her previous visit and replaced them with the fresh set she had, with its rainbow colors.

Etched into Pike's headstone were the words "Always loved and forever missed." He was mostly missed by her. Sharon saved every penny she had to pay for his headstone, and the drug money he had stashed in his apartment provided him with a comfortable eternal resting place.

She sighed deeply as she wiped away the few tears trickling down her face. She planted her knees into the ground and curved over, trying to maintain her composure. She didn't mind staining her pants with grass and dirt, wanting to be as close to him as possible. She'd loved him, and he'd loved her. Her happiness was stolen from her.

"I promise, Pike, I will find the people that did this to you, that put you here, that took you away from me. I will." Her voice cracked, but her heart never wavered.

•••

Sharon Green had come a long way from smoking weed with her friends in a Brooklyn park to busting her ass to make rank in the NYPD from uniformed officer to detective third grade. From the day Pike died, she knew what she had to do. She was going to find and arrest those responsible for his murder.

As she studied and trained at the Academy, her heart went out when she heard about Mona. Hers too was an unsolved murder. When she tried to find her former best friends, Tamar, Cristal, and Lisa, she kept coming up on dead ends. Then, news about Cristal and her family came about—an entire family brutally murdered on Thanksgiving. The carnage was devastating to hear. Unreal. So quickly, things had drastically changed.

Sadly and with a heavy heart, she went to the closed-casket funeral for the murdered family at New Baptist

Church in Brooklyn. The crowd that came to pay their respects was massive. The unspeakable murder of Cristal and her family had been national news for more than a month—children, the elderly, men and women, all shot execution-style in the small Brooklyn apartment like they were casualties of war. New York was sickened by the news, and the country was in shock.

"What monsters could commit such a ghastly crime?" was the question everybody was asking. The city was confused. Two of the alleged gunmen were shot and killed on the scene, leaving the police department scratching its head. The mayor vowed to the public that the remaining killer or killers would be found, tried, convicted, and punished to the fullest extent of the law.

The large church was jam-packed with one thousand people, standing room only, as all members of the community came out in droves to pay their respects to the seventeen closed caskets that lined the stage, from grandmother to grandchild. It seemed like everyone in Brooklyn had come to the funeral, and there wasn't a dry eye in the place.

Sharon looked around for Tamar and Lisa at the funeral, but neither girl was anywhere to be found, which was odd.

Thinking about Cristal's demise along with her family was heartbreaking. If Sharon were a weak woman, she would have broken. But she didn't break. She bent a little, but the pain wasn't enough to snap her in half. In fact, it only made her stronger.

...

She touched the headstone, trying to hold back her tears. Though years had passed since Pike had been gunned down in cold blood, it still felt like yesterday.

"I will always love you," she softly said. She took another deep breath and rose to her feet.

There were so many questions. Did he know his killers? Was it a past beef with someone? What if he had survived? What if he were still alive? Where would she be? Was becoming an NYPD officer her calling?

After a year on the job, Sharon had begun gathering documents on Pike's murder—witness statements, ballistics—anything to help her solve it. As a detective third grade, she had access to a few things and a little legroom to investigate Pike's murder on her own time. The case became as cold as ice, as did Cristal and Mona's murders. All the murders were clean. There was no trace evidence, no solid witnesses, and most importantly, no solid motives. Only speculation. She didn't see any connection between Pike's death and Cristal's and Mona's, but her gut feeling was telling her there was one.

She exited the cemetery and got behind the wheel of her Fiat, where she lingered for a moment. So much was on her mind.

Her service piece, a Glock 19, was holstered on the passenger seat. It had never been fired. Her career in the NYPD had been a cool stint so far—nothing too complicated; no shootouts or life-threatening situations.

She didn't have any wild stories to share with her coworkers, like most experienced officers. She'd made a lot of collars and did her job respectfully, amicably, and with adherence to the rules. She'd started out as a beat cop in the Bronx, and then made patrol with a ten-year veteran who taught her the ropes of the job—the dos and don'ts, and how to survive. Sharon learned fast, and her captain took notice.

She started the ignition. She wanted to cruise through her old neighborhood before going home. Since she'd become a part of the NYPD family, some of the people in her old hood despised her, calling her a pig and a traitor. They wanted nothing to do with her. Others were proud of her accomplishment, that she had actually done something with her life. She was one of the few who'd made it, and that meant a lot to them.

She drove down Pitkin Avenue. The hot July weather brought everyone outside. Hustlers hugged the corners, and crackheads scrounged around for their next hit. Sharon watched as street peddlers lined the sidewalk, moving their illegal CDs, DVDs, and electronics.

Sharon parked and walked into her favorite store, Mike's Chicken and Pizza, nestled on Pitkin Avenue. The weathered green awning was a testament to the shop's longevity. Chicken and pizza was a strange combination for a restaurant to promote, but Mike, a small Italian man that the locals respected, had been around for years and had the best chicken and the best pizza in all of Brownsville and Bed-Stuy. Anyone not familiar with the restaurant usually frowned at fried chicken and pizza being sold together—chicken was soul food, and no Italian had the right to make it better. But Mike's chicken, with its special ingredient, could rival most soul food restaurants.

Sharon walked into the crowded place, its reputation having spread to Queens, Harlem, and even upstate New York. Today, she had a taste for some BBQ chicken. She placed her order and waited near the door, fumbling with her smartphone, checking everyone's latest status on Facebook. As she stood around, she noticed the eyes on her. People who knew her from back in the days gawked at her like she no longer belonged in Brooklyn. But their stares didn't intimidate her. She had come for some food, not to be spotlighted because of her occupation.

As she waited for her order, she looked to her right, and through her peripheral vision she noticed a familiar face. It was Black Earth—Tamar's loud, obnoxious, ghetto mother. Sharon was surprised to see the woman. It had been a long time. The last time she had seen Black Earth, she and Tamar had gotten into it, and cops hauled her off to jail for disorderly conduct.

Sharon observed the husky woman. She had seen better days. Her clothes were worn and old, her long weave looked unkempt, and her cheekbones looked caved in. She looked like she was on some kind of drug, crack maybe.

Tossing her smartphone back into her pocket, Sharon hurried after Black Earth as she trekked down the sidewalk, following her like the professional investigator she'd been trained to be. *Maybe she has an idea where Tamar is.*

Black Earth slid into the lobby of a four-story building at the end of the block, and Sharon was right behind her, forgetting about the order she'd placed at Mike's.

Sharon walked into the building lobby and caught Black Earth disappearing into the stairway. She moved like a cat trying to catch a mouse. She could hear Black Earth climbing the stairs, her breathing heavy like an asthma patient's. She was out of shape and not hard to miss.

Black Earth arrived on the fourth floor and moved down the narrow hallway and knocked on an apartment door with a sense of urgency. Sharon was close behind and watched her from the stairway door. It was obvious to her what Black Earth was there for.

A young, shirtless thug opened the brown apartment door up. "You back again?" he said to her roughly.

"Yeah," Black Earth answered, her tone gentle.

"You got my money?"

Black Earth nodded. She showed him a clump of dollar bills, and he snatched it from her.

"Next time, you call a nigga first," he told her as he served her some drugs.

Black Earth quickly pivoted away from the scowling thug. As she came Sharon's way, Sharon stepped back from the stairway door and waited to confront her.

When the stairway door opened up and Black Earth came into her view, Sharon said, "Black Earth."

Startled, Black Earth spun around, looking at her with wild eyes, ready to attack Sharon like she was an enemy. "What the fuck! Don't be muthafuckin' sneakin' up on me, bitch!"

"It's me, Sharon. You remember me, Tamar's friend?" Sharon said quickly.

Sharon was already on the defensive, not knowing how Black Earth would react. She was known to have violent outbursts. She had her gun and shield on her and kept a safe distance from the woman, and her hand near her Glock, just in case the conversation went sour.

"Aren't you a cop?"

"Yes."

Black Earth went from looking angry to worried. She tried to hide the vials of crack in her hand, wrapping her arm around her stout frame.

Sharon told her, "Don't worry, I'm not here to arrest you."

"Then what are you here for?"

"Tamar. When was the last time you saw her?"

"I don't talk to that bitch," Black Earth spat. Her relationship with her daughter was still strained after Tamar, Cristal, Lisa, and Mona jumped her.

"When was the last time you talked to her?"

"She don't come around much, and when she do, she takes her sisters and brother on these nice shopping sprees, flossing her fuckin' money, buying them nice, expensive things. I gave birth to that stingy bitch, and she don't give me a fuckin' dime."

"Shopping sprees?"

"Yeah."

"Where did she get the money?"

"I don't fuckin' know, but that bitch is rollin' in the dough. That bitch flossin' her money in front of my face, tryin' to be spiteful. I push her out my pussy and look how she do me."

Sharon had heard enough. "Look, here's my number. Whenever you see her, please tell her to give me a call. It's important."

Sharon handed Black Earth her card, and she reluctantly took it. "Tamar is bad news. She's an evil, evil bitch now."

"I would still like to have a word with her."

"I hope you fuckin' arrest that bitch."

"Arrest her?" Sharon was baffled. "For what?"

Black Earth smirked. She charged down the stairway.

Sharon stood in the stairway. She thought about the shopping sprees Tamar was taking her siblings on, and where the money could be coming from. *Did she hook up with a drug dealer, or is she selling drugs?* She took out her notepad and jotted down everything Black Earth had said to her. She didn't have a clue what her former friend was into, but she was determined to find the switch and turn on the lights.

THREE

••••••••••••••••••••••••••••••••••••

Melissa Chin, AKA Daisy, felt like the queen of England as she sat at the head of the table in Mr Chow on 57th Street. Her guests praised the success of her newest book, which was selling fast and moving in extraordinary numbers. Melissa Chin was becoming a big name fast. The people seated at the white cloth table with candlelight had no idea she was a fraud. They kissed her ass and spoiled her with adulation and compliments, and she was eating it all up.

Daisy sipped on pricey champagne and looked like a glamorous brat with high-end clothing, shoes, and handbag.

"How do you do it, Melissa, write the way you do?" Janice asked. "Your stories are vibrant, the characters seem so real, and the plot just jumps out at you. If the books weren't fiction, I might think some of these things actually happened."

Daisy smiled, the compliments stroking her ego. "I'm just born with a gift, you know. Beyoncé sings, I write. I'm like the Beyoncé of the book world. I got what it takes to capture people's attention with my words, you know. Nobody can fuck with my pen game."

"That's right, nobody can fuck wit' my bitch," Janice said loudly. The groupie showed off her curvaceous figure in a low-cut dress and five-inch stilettos. "We are here to enjoy our girl's success and meet us some fine-ass men in the city. If they ain't paid and cute, with something nice between their thighs, then we don't need 'em."

Daisy laughed.

The girls dined on chicken satay and ginger lobster and downed champagne and wine like water. They made their presence known inside the restaurant with the large tips Daisy left. Occasionally patrons would turn their heads at the group of women dining close by and scoff at them.

Daisy loved talking about herself and her career. She ran her mouth about everything.

"You know they trying to offer me a multimillion-dollar book deal for my next joint and it ain't even written yet." *Yeah, bitches, look at me.*

"You serious?"

"Would I lie?"

"I wish I was you."

"I know. My shit stay on fleek," Daisy replied flatly. "And they talking about a movie deal for my first book. You know I can play my own character in the movie, because I'm multitalented."

"Facts," Denise said.

"So tell us, what's your next book going to be about?" Bonnie asked.

"Girl, it's gonna be better than my first two."

Daisy had no idea what the next book would be about. She hadn't seen it yet, nor read the synopsis. The real Melissa Chin hadn't disclosed any details about it, or when it was going to be finished or released.

She sat there with a sure smile on her face. "It's a work in progress. I can't tell y'all about the story, and y'all know I'm under a confidentiality contract."

"Can you just give us a little clue?" Bonnie said. "Tandi and Olivia are ruthless. They got Brooklyn on fire. The books are so good. I'm just addicted to the story."

Daisy grinned, hiding her ineptness. There was nothing to give, because she didn't know what to give and had no idea how her ghostwriter would continue the fourth installment of the series, the long-awaited third installment of the series having just been released. She could only talk about the books published already. She took her time reading the galleys sent to her from the publisher to avoid making a complete fool of herself at book signings across the country.

She was coached to be authentic at press conferences, book signings, and radio interviews. One mistake and it could all go Milli Vanilli. When asked where the story originated, she was trained to say, "It's been building up inside of me for years now. I'm into James Bond films and spy movies, and I love a good conspiracy story."

The world believed she was the creator of the famed characters Tandi and Olivia—two Harlem girls who went from the bottom to the top via murder for hire. They were the Killer Dolls, female terminators more deadly than Cataleya Restrepo from *Colombiana*, Samantha Caine played by Geena Davis in *The Long Kiss Goodnight*, or Uma Thurman in *Kill Bill*.

Daisy continued to bluff an answer to Bonnie's question. It was great that she was a fan, but the bitch was becoming an irritant. She downed the last of her champagne, letting it swirl down her throat.

"Look, Bonnie, like everyone else, you're gonna have to wait until I'm done to find out what happens. I can't be showing you any favoritism in here. And, besides, you talk too fuckin' much. You might get me sued. Don't forget, I am under contract."

Bonnie backed off, pouting.

"Anyway, where we going tonight?" Daisy asked with glee in her tone.

"Anywhere," Denise said. "Where the cuties are at?"

Janice told them, "I think Cheaters is popping tonight, or Mavericks on Fifth Avenue."

"Ooooh," Bonnie uttered. "I heard Mavericks be jumping."

It was Daisy's choice to pick the club. She was the alpha female in the group. She had the money and name. If she told them to jump, they would ask how high.

"I don't know. I feel like Cheaters tonight," she said slowly, looking at Bonnie.

"Yeah, I feel like Cheaters too," Bonnie quickly agreed.

"I know you do."

Daisy was sometimes unkind and sardonic to her friends. She was far from affable when it came to socializing, only putting on a smile and polite mannerisms around people who could help her career and book sales. At the end of the day, she was a complete bitch.

While everyone was itching to go, Daisy wasn't rushing for anyone. It was her day, her career, and without her, her stuck-up and uppity friends wouldn't be experiencing the five-star restaurants, partying in VIP, and cruising around Manhattan in high-end cars.

They remained patient, hiding away their grievances while going into their third hour at Mr Chow.

As Daisy was about to sink her teeth into a large scoop of lime sorbet, she paused, staring at the fine specimen of a man entering the restaurant. Immediately, she recognized his face and felt her panties get moist seeing him.

Domencio was a retired drug distributor turned businessman. Daisy's eyes were transfixed on him as he stood clad in a sharp three-piece double-breasted suit with fancy cufflinks, sparkling Rolex and pinky ring, and dark designer frames. He looked like a celebrity without the entourage. Standing at an even six feet with skin the color of Hershey's milk chocolate, Domencio had thick, jet-black hair with piercing blue-gray eyes, a square jawline, and bulging muscles.

It didn't take long for the girls to turn around to see what suddenly had their friend's attention. He caught their attention too. He had come with a male friend, an associate of his. The men were quickly seated almost at arm's length away from Daisy and her friends.

Domencio, a black man with some Spanish heritage, was one of the most dangerous men in the city. His face had been in numerous newspapers for many crimes and murders, but he had been tried and acquitted. In his mid-forties now, he had become the "Teflon Don" of the city. He spoke Spanish fluently, along with some Italian, and was smart enough to trade the drug game for a legit hustle.

Daisy said to her friends, "You know who that is?"

"No. Who?" Bonnie asked.

"He is fine though," Denise blurted out.

"That's Domencio, a retired gangster and drug dealer. Now he runs a big real estate company in the city. Plus, he owns that club Shuffles on the West Side."

"For real?"

"Yes." Daisy couldn't take her eyes off of him.

Right away, their waiter brought a $1,500 bottle of champagne to their table. Domencio sat in his seat like a don. His swagger was born, not learned.

Daisy grinned. "I feel myself getting pregnant by just looking at him."

Her girls laughed.

Domencio glanced their way for a moment. He happened to smile Daisy's way, and she ate it up. She felt her breathing become thin, and butterflies did gymnastics in her stomach.

"Ooh, he's looking at you, Daisy," Janice said.

"I know."

"Go over and say hi to him," Denise suggested.

Daisy didn't know how to introduce herself to him. She was never nervous around men, but Domencio was an exception. The delicious sorbet she was about to enjoy no longer interested her. She had her eyes on a different kind of dessert, something chocolate with a little more flavor.

"I need to use the bathroom," she said, pushing her chair back from the table.

She felt giddy while passing Domencio and his friend. She gave him a fleeting look and hurried by their table. As she passed, she could feel his eyes on her, knowing he was watching her walk. She was hoping he liked what he saw.

Daisy went into the bathroom to check on her image. She gazed at her reflection, touched up her makeup, fixed a few loose strands of her hair, and did a line of cocaine before exiting the bathroom fifteen minutes later.

While heading back to her table, she so happened to bump into Domencio in a soft collision near the restrooms. She stumbled a little, but he was there to help her.

"I'm so sorry," she quickly apologized, looking nervously at him.

"No, I'm the one that should be apologizing. It's my fault. I got a little distracted."

Daisy locked eyes with him and couldn't turn away. He was more handsome up close and personal. His voice was deep and brooding, and he also had an infectious smile that radiated charm.

"I know you," he said, wagging his index finger at her.

She was taken aback. "You do?"

"Yes. Your face . . . it's familiar," he said evenly. "You're that writer about them girls, the Killer Dolls, if I'm not mistaken."

She smiled. "I'm guilty as sin."

"I love your work."

"You're a fan?"

"An admirer."

She smiled heavily.

"I'm Domencio Partlow."

"Melissa Chin."

"Melissa Chin, you are truly a beautiful woman and a gifted writer."

"Thank you." She blushed. "So, you come here often?" she asked, not knowing what else to say to him.

"It's one of my favorite places to eat."

"Well, it's becoming one of mine now," she replied.

Domencio walked her back to her table and was introduced to her friends. The pair flirted and tried to trump the other with their achievements. He bragged about his everything, and she bragged about her everything. It almost seemed like they were made for each other.

It didn't take long for Daisy's plans to change. Instead of going to the club with her girls, she was taking him home for a good fuck. She had no problem ditching friends for a piece of dick.

Domencio eventually picked up their check and left with her, though he had a baby mama waiting for him at home that night.

•••

Domencio reached out to caress Daisy's face, and she took his hands and placed them on the back of her head, letting him know it was okay to guide her action.

The next several minutes, she concentrated on sucking the head of his dick, using her lips around the crown, tickling the underside with the tip of her tongue. She wanted to make him feel so good. It wasn't every day she got into bed with a handsome criminal mastermind turned multimillionaire. She slammed his big dick into her mouth and he grunted, guiding her head down on his dick, making her deep-throat it.

Daisy would have been contented with just giving him head, but when he told her to sit on his face, she was ecstatic.

He took his thumbs and spread her pussy walls wide and slid his tongue in her sweet spot, and she began grinding her hips rhythmically as he sucked and nibbled on her clitoris for a good long time.

"Fuck me now, baby."

He leaned her over, face down into the pillow, ass arched, legs spread slightly, put on a Magnum, and rammed his meaty dick inside of her. He clamped his hand around her slim waist and fucked her vigorously, opening her pussy up like a good book.

Daisy backed it up on his hard dick, taking it deeply into her. A passionate moan of pleasure escaped her lips. The bliss engulfed him, and as he leaned forward to kiss her, her dripping pussy saturated his entire lower half.

As she rocked, he pushed deeper into her. And they fucked faster and harder.

Moments later, they both came into glory.

Daisy lay nestled in his arms on the wrinkled purple silk sheets, and for the moment, life was good. She had no complaints.

FOUR

●●●●●●●●●●●●●●●●●●●●●●●●●●●●●●●●●

The shower was Cristal's temporary haven. The running water cascaded off her light brown skin as she stood with her head down and eyes closed, her hands palming the Dove soap, wishing she could wash away her pain and her scars. Looking into the bathroom mirror every day served as a constant reminder that her entire family had been slaughtered right in front of her eyes.

That day was supposed to be a joyous occasion. Cristal had so much to be thankful for— family, love, and the new baby on the way—and within the blink of an eye, that was all snuffed out. The betrayal was heartrending, and the loss was devastating.

Cristal could never forget. She could never erase the pain and bloodshed from her mind. It had been seared into her memory. She felt empty and cold. She thirsted for revenge, yearning to cut open her enemies' insides and twist their intestines with her fist and watch them die slowly.

She tried not to think about that fateful day she lost Hugo, the love of her life, her grandmother Hattie, her mother, cousins, aunts, uncles, and most tragically, her unborn child. The Commission had taken everything away from her because she was cocky enough to break the rules.

As the water crashed against her naked skin, she methodically circled her wounds while her eyes remained closed. One hole was stitched together right under her rib cage, and the other wound was one inch away from her heart.

It had been three years since she had taken two body shots from a high-powered firearm and another two shots to her face that disfigured her and changed her entire life. Not only did she lose her family, she lost her beauty too.

Daisy was right about one thing. Her face, as she saw it now, couldn't sell much of anything. One bullet had grazed her skull, leaving behind a deep keloid scar, and the second bullet grazed her left cheek and took off a portion of her left earlobe. Tamar's betrayal had done a number on her.

The doctors had said that she was lucky to be alive, which she thought was an understatement. The incident left her bitter and angry.

While she was healing and hidden away from society and the danger, she wrote about her pain, camouflaging her feelings and her anger into a full-length novel, holding nothing back, substituting her tragedy with fictional characters. Writing the book was somewhat therapeutic, but it couldn't fully heal her from the agony and sadness. But it was a start.

Seeing blood spill would have been a better start, but Cristal needed time to think and to heal. She also needed time to methodically plot out her revenge.

Her story was being read by millions of people, and unbeknownst to her readers, the Commission was being exposed. Daisy was the perfect foil to launch her book, to sell her tragedy, but the fame had gone to her head. Daisy believed that she wasn't expendable, but she was about to learn a hard lesson. Nothing lasts forever.

Cristal thought really hard about Daisy. She really wanted to have some remorse for the young girl, but the bitch was likely to compromise everything.

She finished showering and stepped onto the white-tiled floor. She toweled off and then knotted the towel by her breasts. She stepped out of the bathroom and walked around her spacious Boston apartment. The day she became a deadly assassin was the beginning of her end. She had so many names floating around in her head, so many identities in her possession, she was never herself. Not since her "murder." Most days she didn't know who she was. One day she was Elizabeth, the next she was Melissa or Lara or Caitlyn, and the list went on and on. If the Commission knew she was still alive, they would hunt her down to the end of the earth.

After donning a long white T-shirt that draped down to her knees, Cristal went into her bedroom, dropped her knees against the parquet floor, and reached under the bed to grip the leather black handle to a large black suitcase. She pulled it into her view; it was big enough to hide a small body. Next, she went to her closet and grabbed a large wheeled trunk.

She carried the suitcase and rolled the trunk into the next room. Her apartment was bare like her soul, sparsely furnished, with no pictures or other personal touches to liven the place up. She sank into the folding chair and removed every piece of weaponry, and within a short time, she had her own personal gun show displayed across the table—two black .45 ACPs, a Glock 19, two Smith & Wesson SW99 .9mms, a .38 Special, three .9mm Berettas, and two stainless .45s. It looked like she had broken into a military armory and hit the jackpot.

She also had i the Mossberg 500 12-gauge and an FN Tactical Police 12-gauge, along with a Heckler & Koch G36C 5.56mm, a Heckler & Koch HK91A3, an SIG SG 552, and two of her most powerful guns, a Remington 700 PSS and a Barrett M82, both of which could dismember limbs and blow holes the size of basketballs in muthafuckas.

Cristal was a trained markswoman. The Commission had taught her how to kill, and she perfected the art. She knew how and when to be discreet and when to be messy, to send a message.

It was going to be a long night. She was determined to clean all her guns properly, taking care of her babies like they were her kids. She had everything she needed placed in front of her—cleaning solvent, lubricant, a bore brush, a cleaning rod, and cotton swabs.

She placed a special CD in the CD drive of her small stereo, and opera music started to play in the background.

Luciano Pavarotti's tenor voice started to blare into the room, the song of choice, "Miss Sarajevo." Listening to opera was a far cry from the rap lyrics she grew up on. Opera was more soothing to her ears.

After the attempt on her life, Cristal was now prone to panic attacks, fits of uncontrollable rage, and loud noise sensitivity. She had to take a cocktail of Xanax, Vicodin, and Zoloft to control it.

One by one, she unloaded her weapons, looked through the barrel from back to front to confirm that there were no rounds in the chamber or stuck in the barrel. Then she dismantled the weapon, removed the firing pin, and went to work on the cold steel like a hospital surgeon, cleaning each gun meticulously and reloading it.

Three hours later, every weapon was cleaned, shining, and looking brand-new. She was ready to put them to use.

•••

Dressed in all black, Cristal sat covertly parked outside the five-story walk-up in SoHo, Manhattan. The area wasn't busy, being midnight. A few yellow cabs traveled back and forth on the cobblestone street, but the pedestrian traffic was sparse.

It was the perfect place for a woman like Daisy to reside. Besides its unique architectural style, SoHo was a shopping mecca. In the last two decades, SoHo had evolved from an artists' village to a commercial paradise. Walking along the streets, one could pass countless clothing retail stores such as Ralph Lauren, J.Crew, Betsey Johnson, and Tory Burch.

Cristal exited her vehicle without reservation. Her weapon of choice tonight was the .9mm Beretta. She crossed the narrow cobblestone street nestled quietly away from busy Canal and Houston Streets. She moved stealthily toward the building and stood in front of a high storefront window with the fire escape a few feet above her head. She took a deep breath and, using the structure for support, leaped like a cat, her arms outstretched, and grabbed onto the fire escape, using her upper-body strength to pull herself up. She was quiet and fast.

Once on the fire escape, she pulled out the pistol and slowly twisted the long, deadly silencer onto the barrel of the .9mm. She ascended toward the fifth floor and came to Daisy's living-room window, which was slightly open. Everything looked copasetic, with no noisy neighbors, no noise coming from within, and the street below her looking tranquil.

She slid into the apartment, adjusted her eyes to the darkness inside, and made her way from the open window into the apartment, her gun gripped in her hand. She saw a speck of light creeping from the hallway leading toward the bedroom. Cristal walked ahead, her .9mm stretched out in front of her, leading the charge. Her training had taught her how to move in silence. Almost like a feather blowing in the wind, she didn't make a noise.

When she got to the bedroom door, she pressed her ear to the door and listened. Nothing. She crouched closer to the floor and carefully pushed open the door, slightly enough where there was little notice of any movement, and crept into the bedroom, low to the floor.

Asleep in the bed, butt naked, were Daisy and Domencio after a long night of fucking their brains out.

The man was unexpected. *Damn!* Cristal thought. She wanted this killing to be clean.

How in the hell was she supposed to move him? He was all muscles and mass. It was going to be difficult, and she didn't have time to deal with difficult. She was pissed. She thought about killing them both and coming back another day to clean it up. She needed Daisy to disappear. There couldn't be a body. No one could know she was dead.

She frowned at the dilemma in front of her as she watched the two lovebirds sleep peacefully. It would have been easy, a few shots in critical places and done. But moving the bodies would be a bit complicated. Besides, who was the man lying next to Daisy? He could be missed.

Cristal stood over them like a shadow. She decided against it. Daisy's company had caused her life to be spared. She could always come back. Better to return than to complicate an easy thing. So she crept back out of the apartment and waited.

FIVE

● ●

everal hours went by, and there were only two hours before dawn would be lighting up the sky. Still, this particular area of SoHo was quiet like a small town in the Midwest. Cristal had come all the way from Boston, so she wasn't about to fail. She sat patiently behind the wheel of her dark blue Audi. Since the Farm, it had been embedded into her—always take your time, study your mark, know their routine, and become familiar with the surroundings.

As she sat, she suddenly noticed Daisy's male friend exiting the building. She read him. Leaving in the middle of the night the way he did, she imagined he had a girlfriend or wife waiting for him at home. She chuckled.

She watched him climb inside a black BMW 745i and navigate out of the tight parking spot before driving off. Now she could move.

She slid out the car and repeated the same routine as before, climbing up the fire escape, her .9mm in hand, silencer at the end, bullet already in the chamber, and went for the same open window. This time, she had to be extra careful. Maybe Daisy was awake. Either way, she was going to complete her mission.

Cristal effortlessly crept through the window. This time she knew the layout of the apartment. She was trained to have a picture-perfect memory.

This time, she was audacious. No crouching, no moving around in the apartment like a cockroach, knowing Daisy was alone. If confronted, Daisy was no match for her lethal abilities. It would be like a tree going against a hurricane.

Cristal moved toward the bedroom with an unrelenting attitude, her eyes cold slits, her fist clenched around the silver handle of the Beretta. She was ready to show the little bitch the consequences of being greedy. She could hear some movement inside the master bedroom, and a television now turned on low. She noticed the yellow light under the doorway. Cristal lifted her right leg, knee pointed upwards, and thrust it forward, kicking open the bedroom door with a burst of force that startled Daisy.

Immediately, Cristal had the gun trained at her head. "Don't you fuckin' move."

Daisy, still butt naked and seated at the foot of her bed, stared wide-eyed at Cristal clad in black standing in front of her with the barrel of the silencer pointed right between her eyes. Right away, she was overcome with fear. "Please don't kill me," she begged loudly.

"I'm not going to kill you."

"I'm sorry, I didn't mean to—"

"Shut the fuck up!"

Daisy was shaking like a leaf on a windy day. She kept her attention fixed on Cristal and the gun. The tears started to show in her eyes.

"Get up!"

Daisy complied, moving slowly, her whole body trembling from fear. "What are you going to do with me? I'm sorry. I didn't mean to act up at the last book signing. I don't want anything."

Cristal shouted, "I said shut up!"

She made Daisy move around her well-designed bedroom at gunpoint and forced her into the living room. She instructed her to take a seat at the small writing desk that sat cater-corner in the neat living room. Daisy sank her naked ass into the cushioned chair and curved herself over the desk, her whimpering uncontrollable.

Cristal got a pen and some paper from the drawer.

"Please . . . whatever you want, I'll behave. I'm sorry. Just don't hurt me," she said, tears trickling down her face.

"I want you to write something for me," Cristal said.

"Write what?"

"I'll tell you."

Daisy could barely hold the pen steady in her hand, which shook like it was in a California earthquake.

Cristal held the gun pointed to the back of her head. Daisy couldn't help but to nervously glance over her shoulder, wondering what Cristal had planned for her.

Cristal approached closer, placing the tip of the silencer to the back of Daisy's head and said, "I need you to write this down."

Daisy placed the pen to the paper and started jotting down every word Cristal spoke.

"I am saddened to inform my fans and the public that I will no longer be able to make any special appearances at book signings, radio interviews, speaking engagements, or interviews. I have decided to leave the country for a long while and go into seclusion. The reasons for this sudden decision I do not care to disclose at the moment, but they are good reasons. I thank everyone for the love and support they've shown me and know my work will always carry on."

Cristal made Daisy sign it as Melissa Chin.

Immediately, Daisy started to cry out hysterically knowing the inevitable was about to happen to her.

With the gun still pointed at the back of Daisy's head, Cristal said, "Get up!"

"Please! I'm sorry, so sorry. I'll just disappear. I swear I won't be a problem to you. Just let me go. I promise, I'll go back to the Midwest right now."

Keeping Daisy alive was too much of a risk for Cristal. It was inevitable that the Commission would eventually track her down, most likely torture her for information, and kill her.

"Get dressed."

Daisy walked over to her walk-in closet on the opposite side of the bedroom. She slowly opened the narrow double closet doors and walked into what looked like a whirlwind of clothing placed everywhere. She was living the good life, wearing Prada and Gucci, dining in nice restaurants, chilling in VIP in the hottest clubs, and having the best sex with some of the finest men in New York City.

Daisy stood in the middle of her closet looking befuddled.

"Hurry up and put something on," Cristal snapped, becoming impatient with her.

Daisy looked at the tons of clothing she'd collected since becoming Melissa Chin. Her tears continued to trickle down her brown cheeks.

Her nakedness was starting to bother Cristal. She stepped into the closet and decided to choose for her, since Daisy was too dumbfounded. With the barrel of the silencer pushing clothing to the side draping of the hangers, she set her eyes on something.

"I like this," she said. "Put this on."

Daisy didn't argue with her. She slid into the short, colorful Gucci dress.

Cristal pulled Daisy out of the closet, and after she put on a pair of shoes, the two were out the front door. Daisy was being kidnapped. The two exited the building with Daisy still begging for her freedom.

Cristal popped the trunk to her Audi and forced Daisy inside.

"Please, I'll just go away," Daisy begged once again before the trunk slammed shut.

•••

It was just over an hour drive to the designated place in Scarsdale, New York. But with the sprawling sunlight, Cristal didn't have the cover she needed. She needed to wait until it was dark again, so she gagged Daisy and kept her hidden in the trunk until dusk.

When night fell over the Scarsdale neighborhood, Cristal drove near a secluded area of a sprawling cemetery, up a hill, overlooking the community. It was dark and away from traffic or wandering pedestrians.

The grave was already dug. Now it was just a matter of dumping the body and filling it in. There was a crescent moon above, and between the thick shrubberies and tall trees, Cristal had enough cover to kill Daisy.

She parked close to the grave and forced Daisy out of the trunk at gunpoint. Daisy couldn't scream due to the cloth wedged into her mouth. Her wrists were bound tightly, her hair disheveled, and her tear-stained face was still searching for some sympathy from Cristal.

She marched Daisy toward the open grave, and when Daisy saw the gruesome fate that lay ahead of her, she pivoted quickly in her high heels and tried to run.

Suddenly the butt of the Beretta came crashing down against the back of her skull, and she collapsed onto her hands and knees.

"Don't be stupid," Cristal said.

Daisy squirmed and groaned, the dirty white rag shoved into her mouth gagging her and making her incoherent. Her tears continued to fall, her eyes wide with fear. She didn't want to die, but she didn't have a choice.

Cristal forced her to the foot of the open grave.

Daisy was in a full-blown panic. She quivered so much and was so scared, a yellow stream trickled down her inner thigh and made a small puddle where she stood. Her eyes frantically searched for some kind of pardon from her soon-to-be executioner.

Cristal shook her head in disgust. She stepped forward with the gun angled away from Daisy, and removed the gag, allowing her victim to speak her last words. She didn't know why. It would be the only empathy from her that night.

The second she was able to speak, Daisy started to beg for her life again. "Don't do this. I can't die like this. My parents . . . if I die like this, they won't be able to give me a proper burial. If I'm missing, it will kill them not knowing where I am. I ran away from home when I was fifteen." She sobbed loudly.

Cristal didn't give a fuck. It had to be this way. Daisy was Melissa Chin, and she couldn't afford to have Melissa Chin found dead, and then have it subsequently revealed that she was really a young girl from the Midwest named Daisy McLeod. It would be too messy and too much of a risk.

Besides, Cristal quite enjoyed writing. It was cathartic and helped her deal with her past. Cristal would keep producing books, but this time she wouldn't be stupid enough to attach a face to it.

Cristal lifted her eyes to lock with Daisy's. "Sorry it had to be this way."

Before Daisy could yell for help or defend herself, the .9mm was quickly raised to meet her forehead, and a bullet went slamming into her frontal lobe. The impact lifted Daisy off her feet and sent her flying backwards into the deep grave with a loud thump against the dirt. The body landed sideways.

Cristal aimed at the body and fired three more shots. *Poot! Poot! Poot!*

Cristal didn't need to cover the grave completely, for it had already been pre-dug by gravediggers for a funeral early the next morning. She just needed to cover the body with dirt and conceal it enough so tomorrow, when the casket was lowered into the ground during the burial, no one would ever suspect their loved one was sharing their final resting place with someone else.

SIX

● ●

Tamar navigated her black Audi RS 4 convertible through the city streets like a NASCAR driver. The car was sleek, fast, and powerful, and it caught attention—just like her. Her hair was flowing in the wind with the top down, the backdrop becoming a blur as she did 85 on the West Side Highway. Cops didn't concern her. The law didn't apply to her. She had connections and resourceful friends in the right places. When she wasn't a deadly assassin, she found pleasure and comfort in New York's nightlife.

Life had been extremely good to Tamar. She lived in a penthouse suite on the East Side and had two exotic cars to cruise around in the city—the Audi RS 4 and a black-on-black BMW 650i. She had a monthly stipend to burn, jewelry to show off, and designer outfits she only wore once.

The night was young, and she was feeling animated and horny. She wanted something to take home and play with for the night. Man or woman, it didn't matter to her. If they were sexy, voluptuous, or endowed, then they caught her attention.

While speeding on the West Side Highway, heading north, Tamar pulled on her burning cigarette and exhaled. With her Jimmy Choo pressed down on the accelerator, she weaved in and out of traffic like she was in a high-speed chase.

Fifteen minutes later, Tamar pulled up to the Copycat Club in midtown. It was 11 p.m., and the line outside was a half a block long to get inside the popular club.

Tamar pulled up to the valet parking and stepped out of her shining chariot looking exotic in something sheer. Her long legs stretched to the sky in her six-inch shoes. She approached the entrance to the club looking like a diva, all eyes on her.

She strutted toward the entrance where two muscular, brutish-looking bouncers stood. She moved with a fiery grace, her persona oozing dominance and style like no other. The bling she wore was blinding. Diamond teardrops dangled from her ears, and a $90,000 tennis necklace adorned her neck.

Subtly, she slipped a hundred-dollar bill into the meaty palm of one of the bouncers. The velvet rope separating the outside from the inside unhooked as the towering bouncer stepped aside and let her into the club with a smile. She sashayed inside with a blank look.

Copycat was a moneyed club that exemplified elegance through its rich and polished décor. A regal entryway, typically accented with attractive partygoers, set the standard for the entire venue. Inside, the 5000-square-foot space boasted state-of-the-art technology with forty-to seventy-inch LCD flat-screens and VIP suites perched strategically around the club, giving the occupants a bird's-eye view of the dance floor below.

Tamar entered the club where a lavish bar spread around the room, followed by a sunken dance floor. The music was loud, blaring Rihanna's "Pour It Up."

The crowd was hyped as over a hundred revelers crammed onto the sunken dance floor. As Tamar moved through the crowd, she noticed a lot of pretty faces and handsome mugs. They noticed her too. Her tiger walk demanded attention. Men gawked at her, and women too. It seemed like the elite had come out tonight. DJ Flex was rocking the crowd with his flavor of mixes and gaudy sound over the mic.

Up above everyone else was her choice, the VIP area. Whatever club, whatever state, business or pleasure, it was bottle service. She could afford it.

Tamar sat alone in the cushioned VIP and ordered a bottle of Rosé. From her perspective, everyone looked like a potential victim, when it came to carrying out a contract for the Commission. Tamar had no conscience, and she did her job without judgment. She had lost her soul long ago when she'd gunned down Cristal's family, from young to old. She had always been jealous of Cristal ever since she started a relationship with E.P. She wanted the top-ranking position and the power, and was willing to do whatever it took to get it.

It had been three years since that day she'd sold her soul to the devil. They were all dead, Cristal, Lisa, and

Mona. But one friend from her past remained and was asking about her. Sharon. It was surprising to hear that Sharon had become a cop. Who would have thought that?

But why is she asking around about me now? Tamar wondered.

They hadn't seen or spoken to each other or crossed paths in so long. The friendship almost felt ancient between them. Sharon had gone her way, and Tamar had gone hers.

Tamar was now on the opposite side of the law. She remembered gunning down Pike when Sharon had just found love in him. She had no remorse about the hit. She had nothing against the man, but it was business. And if she had to do it all over again, she wouldn't hesitate.

Tamar sipped her Rosé from the flute glass in her hand. From the looks of her, no one could tell she was a stone-cold assassin. She was model beautiful and dressed to kill in her sheer dress. Even DJ Flex casually eyed her from his perch in the DJ booth across the room. A pretty young thing, alone, paying for bottle service in VIP made a strong statement.

Usually, she was about business, watching and reading her victims, familiarizing herself with their lives without them knowing she even existed, and then striking with the speed and skill of a venomous snake. But tonight, it was pleasure only. No one's blood would spill tonight.

She stood up from her seat and walked toward the glass railing, one manicured hand lightly gripping the structure, the flute in the other. She gazed down and tried to search for something that caught her eye. Her pussy throbbed for some action. Lately, she had been so busy with work that she hadn't had any time to treat herself.

She searched through the sea of people dancing, drinking, and grinding. She downed the champagne, set the glass aside, and made her way down toward the packed dance floor. She wanted to join in on the fun.

The dance floor was dimmed, and Chris Brown and throwback Wu-Tang Clan were playing loudly throughout the club. She paraded through the tight crowd and positioned herself in the middle of the dance floor. She threw her arms and hands up, transitioning into party mode, moving slowly and nicely to the beat, snapping her fingers, swaying her hips from side to side. She had rhythm and style. Her movement was like a mating dance to gain attention from either sex.

It didn't take long for a pair of masculine hands to touch her sides gently. Her back was to the invader trying to position himself behind her backside. She felt his groin push against her, locking his body into hers.

She had to get a glimpse of him. If he was fine, he had a chance. If he wasn't, then she wouldn't be shy about telling him off. So far, from what she felt from behind her, she knew he was tall. As he gyrated his pelvis against her thick backside, she pivoted slightly to get a good look at him, and what she saw didn't turn her off. In fact, he was a handsome, well dressed black male with a fit, muscular build. Clad in a black fitted shirt and black slacks, his movement against her was precise.

She spun around to face him, taking in his full height. He was six one with a tapered haircut and a thick, dark goatee sprucing his full lips. His onyx eyes were attractive, and the scent of his cologne was intoxicating.

"What's your name, beautiful?" he spoke into her ear, his voice competing with the blaring music inside the club.

Tamar smiled, thinking, *He'll do.* "Jenny."

"I'm Mitchell. Can I buy you a drink?"

"You can."

Their dance together was brief. They moved through the crowd toward the sweeping bar.

Tamar read him quickly. From the block, Brooklyn probably. His wardrobe was simply put together, his jewelry from Pitkin or Jamaica Avenue, his swag, a nigga from the block trying to play Casanova. But he couldn't compete with her. He was one-dimensional, while she was three.

"What you drinking?" he asked.

"Martini. Shaken, not stirred."

"I got you."

He signaled for the bartender and pulled out his wad of cash, desperately wanting to make an impression. His cash was inferior, as was his intelligence. She needed him for one thing only—sex. Though his conversation was engaging, he wasn't articulate. Tamar couldn't help but to think, if she'd met him before training on the Farm, working for the Commission, making her money, she would have fallen head over heels in love with him. But her mind had long been set adrift from fools like him.

He paid for her martini, sipped on his Corona, and they lingered by the bar, talking.

"I saw you in VIP alone, popping bottles. I like that shit, a woman doing her own thing. You come here often?"

"I don't. You?"

"I come with my peoples."

"Your peoples? Girlfriend?" she asked, as if it mattered to her.

"No, no girlfriend. I'm single."

Mitchell couldn't keep his eyes off Tamar, scoping her body from head to toe, making his intentions obvious. She smiled. She flirted. He was transparent. She fed into his bullshit, knowing he was a more than a few steps down from E.P.

•••

Tamar and E.P. were an odd couple, if you could call them a couple. She had fallen in love with him, and she missed him. She continually wanted to prove herself to him. They had been fucking since Cristal's death. At first, it was just rough sex between them—back shots, in the ass, raw dog wherever and whenever. But then, for Tamar, it transitioned into something more, with her catching feelings and falling in love.

In the beginning, she wanted what Cristal had, the respect, his admiration, and his heart. She wanted E.P. to back her, show her favoritism, and help her become known in the underworld. He had that type of pull, the clout to take her to the next level.

But as weeks turned into months, and months turned into years, with Tamar not having any substance, or anyone of substance in her life, she began to latch onto him. She was always dreaming about him sneaking into her bedroom in the wee hours of the night to fuck her. She would yearn for him to stay until the morning, but he never allowed sunlight to catch him in her bed.

Tamar knew that E.P. missed Cristal. It showed in his actions with him sometimes feeling remorseful over what he had done to her. He had reacted on emotion when he found out she was serious about a low-class, low-life drug pusher. It disturbed him deeply. He was educated, distinguished, and handsome. He felt his lovemaking was solid and that he had a lot to offer. So why would Cristal stray away to someone else?

Being rejected by Cristal had sent him over the edge, and he sanctioned the hit that the Commission didn't authorize. Only to himself would he admit that he'd gone too far without hearing her side of the story first. Now he and Tamar were in too deep, violating all the rules with their sexual relations and sins, and they had to plug the gaping wound before it got even bigger.

•••

Tamar smiled in Mitchell's face, looking innocent like a swimming dolphin. She continued sipping on her martini and making decent conversation with him. She had killed men like him over a dozen times across the country. In fact, as he talked, she visualized various ways of hypothetically taking him down. Poison maybe, or a quick thrust from a sharp blade into his heart; he wouldn't even see it coming. But he wasn't a mark, and she wasn't being paid to spill his blood.

Uninterested in any more casual talk, she downed her martini and blurted out to Mitchell, "Let's cut the bullshit—You wanna leave here and fuck?"

He grinned heavily, somewhat taken aback by her abrupt approach. Her eyes whispered to him that she was serious. "It's your world, beautiful," he replied simply, ready to leave with her.

•••

Tamar walked into her spacious penthouse apartment on the East Side, and Mitchell followed inside behind her. The minute she flipped the switch and brought light into the place, Mitchell's jaw almost hit the floor.

"Damn! You living like this?"

She smiled and continued to walk farther into her residence, smoothly slipping out of her dress, letting it fall to the floor, revealing the black thong that sank into the crack of her ample butt cheeks. She made her way toward the master bedroom. Her actions were clear as day— she wanted some dick.

While Mitchell was still in awe at the full-floor, three-bedroom, two-and-one-half-bath loft with a wraparound planted terrace and soaring ceilings in the living and dining room, Tamar was already in the bedroom wondering if he was coming or not.

"Yeah, I'm gonna definitely like fucking you," he said, undoing his pants and walking toward the bedroom.

Moments later, he joined her on the bed. He put her breasts together, sucking both nipples at the same time. He licked and sucked the underside of her tits. She gave him a definite invitation, her legs spreading again and again and again. She was soaking wet, humping herself against his thigh and desperate for things to proceed much faster. She wasn't that kind of bitch. She wasn't for the lovemaking, passionate kissing, and slow grinding. She liked her sex rough, fast, and hard and wanted the nigga to be crude and aggressive right off the bat.

He went down low, sucking on her pussy and ramming his tongue against her clit, enjoying the way she tasted.

Tamar wrapped her legs around him, clamping him into an unmovable position.

Mitchell was surprised at how strong she was. It felt like she could break his neck with one simple motion.

"Ooooh, suck on that pussy," she groaned.

His tongue went inside her deep, bringing Tamar into a state of disbelief that he was so adept at pleasing her. She had made a wise choice.

He licked her sensitive button and felt her thighs tighten around his head. Mitchell slid his fingers inside her wet hole, making her buck that much harder, moan that much louder. He used his lips on her wet clit, making it his mission to make her explode in his mouth.

"Don't stop. Ugh. Ooooh, don't stop. Right there."

Tamar grabbed his head and held it to her mound, not allowing him to move at all.

Then she pulled her legs back to her chest, giving him an invitation to fuck the shit out of her. He rose up, rolling a Magnum condom back onto his thick, eight-inch length. He was ready to feel that pussy. He aimed his dick at the place he needed to be, pushed the head of his dick in her pussy, and then they both cried out, Tamar's eyes rolling back in her head.

Mitchell got into a rhythm quickly, steady and deep. Her pussy gripped him. He was in a trance. Her nails dug into his flesh, and they fucked vigorously with his length ramming into her cervix over and over.

Tamar purred her approval, her eyes closed, with Mitchell heavily on top of her, thrusting himself between her open legs.

"Mmmm, yeah! That feels good. Harder, nigga. Fuck me harder!"

They both were unaware of the figure suddenly in the room with them. It was like he appeared out of nowhere. He stood a few feet from the bed, gazing at the nigga's hairy ass and their sexual tryst. He looked at the two of them with an emotionless stare. He extended his right arm with the hefty Desert Eagle gripped in his fist and the suppressor at the end. He pulled the trigger.

Poot!

The bullet tore through the back of Mitchell's head. The large caliber of the gun made the back of his head explode like a firecracker going off. There was a slight,

"Oomph!" coming from the victim, as his blood discharged over the bed and Tamar's naked body. His body collapsed against her, dead and with a hole the size of a baseball in the back of his head.

"Playtime's over!" the killer said gruffly.

He stood over them like the Grim Reaper, his eyes cold as ice. He was impassive about his action, looking like a genetically engineered hit man.

Tamar was doused with Mitchell's blood, but she didn't panic. "What the fuck, E.P.?"

She evenly pushed the body off of her, placing Mitchell on his back, sprawled out in her queen-size bed and very expensive sheets. She stood up.

E.P. lowered the gun. "Had fun?"

"Until you fucked it up."

"Where you find him?"

"The club. Why? You jealous?" she asked, smirking.

While Tamar stood stark naked in front of him, trying to clean off Mitchell's blood, E.P. tossed a book on the bed, catching Tamar's attention.

"It's her latest novel," he said.

Tamar was aware of the book and its contents. Reading these books made her blood boil and her knees quiver. She had been assigned the case and was no closer to getting at Melissa Chin than when she'd started.

"We got a serious problem, and you're out here having casual fucks?"

"A girl is allowed to have some fun. You stopped fucking me."

"Not when she has an assignment. And you're no closer to finding and exterminating this bitch."

"I'll find her. I always do."

E.P. stepped closer, the gun still in his hand. It wasn't a threat to her yet, being by his side, the muzzle pointed toward the floor. His eyes focused intently on her. "You've had this murdergram for a while now, and still no results. The Commission is becoming very uneasy with your performance."

"The Commission has no need to worry about anything. My earlier performances precede me. Haven't I always fulfilled a contract?"

"Reminder, you're only as good as your last job. And you can always be replaced."

Tamar didn't like what she was hearing from him.

E.P. gazed at the body before him. Mitchell's blood was soaking into the sheets, little by little dripping onto the parquet floor like a leaky faucet. It wouldn't be long before the body went into rigor mortis. The man meant nothing to him; it was as easy to him as squashing a fly.

For a moment, he veered off the subject. "Does he fuck you better than me?"

Tamar smiled. "Nobody fucks me better than you."

He slowly turned his attention away from the body like he was some machine and looked at Tamar coldly. "I don't want this happening again," he said to her in a low monotone.

"You serious? You don't want me, but I can't fuck anybody else?"

"It interferes with your perception."

"Perception? I'm still a flesh-and-blood woman with needs."

"Needs? If this hit doesn't get carried out, your needs are going to be the least of your problems."

She frowned. "You're no fun anymore," she said. E.P. was making her feel as if her life was in danger if she didn't complete her murdergram.

"Read the book, and kill this bitch."

E.P. pivoted on his clean-looking shoes and made his exit, leaving Tamar holding the bag. Now she had a body to dispose of, and she hadn't even come yet.

SEVEN

●●●●●●●●●●●●●●●●●●●●●●●●●●●●●●●●●●●●

Cristal sat at the famous Boston Cafe having a mocha latte and reading *The New York Times*. As usual, she had on huge dark shades and a black seaside sunhat with a flower pinned to its side pulled low over her brow to cover her features. She was discreet and quiet, enjoying the sunny day and cool moment.

Boston was so different from New York. It felt like a town full of businesspeople during the day and college kids at night. One of the oldest and most historic cities in North America, it had a very European feel and tried to preserve all its history. Like New York, it was very densely packed and visitor-friendly, with great public transportation. The streets were winding with many dead ends and one-ways, not to mention hyper-aggressive drivers and reckless jaywalkers.

The café was thin with customers and foot traffic in the late morning, it being a working day. Traffic on I-90 was flowing like a river stream.

Sitting at the sidewalk café with its wrought-iron chairs and glass-top table, Cristal reflected on Daisy for a moment, retracing her steps in her head. She wanted to make sure she didn't make any mistakes.

•••

After burying Daisy, she went back to the SoHo apartment and wiped it clean during the middle of the night. The Farm had taught her how to clean up a crime scene, leaving no prints or DNA. Plus, the fact that Daisy wasn't murdered there meant no body, no crime.

She had swept away any trace evidence, packed everything Daisy owned—clothes, shoes, and her identification and so on—and threw it into the trunk of her car. While going through the apartment, Cristal had stumbled upon a couple of credit cards and a loan application that Daisy had applied for in Melissa Chin's name.

Stupid bitch! Cristal said to herself.

She wasn't the brightest. Melissa Chin was denied because the renowned author didn't actually exist. It was a pseudonym.

Cristal shook her head at Daisy's ignorance. She had become greedy. And if she wanted to spare Daisy's life, it was possible—make her go back home to the Midwest maybe. But she had to kill her.

Cristal knew that sooner or later, it would get back to the Commission that someone was exposing all their secrets via books, telling about the intense training on the Farm, the church, the individuals responsible for taking nobodies off the streets and converting them into

trained assassins. Writing those books was one of many
bad decisions that could cost Cristal her life yet again, but
somehow writing those three novels helped her heal and
deal with the tragedy.

Cristal had lived in anonymity for a long while, being
extra careful with the name Melissa Chin. As far as the
world knew, Cristal was dead. She knew it would only
be a matter of time before the Commission found Daisy.
Thankfully, Daisy was dead.

•••

While Cristal sat in front of the commercial
establishment, a FedEx truck pulled up on the block and
parked. The driver, a tall, chubby black male, filled out his
uniform completely. He whistled while carrying packages
in and out of the businesses, his tan skin dripping with
sweat as he lifted heavy boxes in the summer heat.

Soon after his job delivering to everyone else was
done, he casually walked Cristal's way. "Excuse me," he
said softly. "Ms. Centaur?"

Cristal looked up at the man and smiled weakly at
him. Centaur, which meant half man, half horse in Greek
mythology, was her code name from her new agency.
She'd chosen that name because she felt like a hybrid—a
cross between the woman she wanted to be—a wife and
mother—and the woman she was—an assassin.

"Yes?"

"I have a package for you that I need you to sign for."

He passed her the envelope, and she quickly signed for it.

He smiled. "Have a nice day." He turned and went to his truck, leaving Cristal with her new murdergram.

She didn't open it in public. Instead, she shoved it down into her bag, mixing it with the other contents inside, and quietly finished drinking her latte. She headed home a half-hour later.

•••

Back in the comforts of her cozy apartment, Cristal closed her blinds and went into her bedroom. Before kicking off her heels and getting really comfortable, she tore open the package and tilted it over her bed. A 128-GB flash drive dropped from it. She pulled out her Mac computer, placed the flash drive into her USB port, and uploaded the information.

With the stroke of the "Enter" key, a videogram came up. Cristal sat at the foot of her bed waiting for her information to come up. At first the video was represented with different-sized key frames packed in a visually pleasing form, reminiscent of a comic book. And then gradually the key frames came together into one image across her computer screen. The clip was scaled to fill the screen exactly. A man appeared on her 15-inch screen. His face and voice was distorted, but everything else around him was clear as day.

In her videograms, there was always a man, an imposing figure seated behind a massive desk in a room decorated with deep, rich, solid wood, high-end artwork, and a lit pipe in a nearby ashtray in what appeared to be in a somewhat stylized environment. She had never seen his full face. She'd never met anyone from the agency she had joined. It was all indirect—her instructions, contracts, and missions. She felt like a character from *Charlie's Angels*, but instead of being part of a private investigation firm, she was with an agency of some of the best contract killers around.

"Hello, Centaur," the distorted voice and warped image greeted. *"Your assignment is Chinese diplomat, Chow Ling Tao."*

Two clear split-screen images of Chow Ling Tao came up on her screen. The image on the left had Chow Ling Tao, dressed sharply in a dark, three-piece suit decorated with medals and military insignias, associating with some high officials at a formal event in the United States. The image on the right showed him fully clad in a ceremonial uniform—an open-neck coat with picked lapel and square laps, two lower insert pockets with flap, tooth-edges at collar edge, sleeve cuffs, and outseams on his trousers.

Cristal listened carefully and seared the man's image into her memory. The man continued informing Cristal about her target, who allegedly had been stealing U.S. secrets for years. He was from a small town on the outskirts of Beijing. He had always been protected because of his rank, influence, and power. But he'd until he stopped selling his intel to the Chinese government and struck a deal with the Russians. Now China had hired Cristal's agency to dispose of the problem.

"You have one week to complete this task," was all the man said.

When the videogram footage ran out, it was programmed to automatically erase itself. Cristal had already memorized everything. The information she received was adequate. He would be in New York in a few days to attend a charity event at the Lincoln Center, where she planned on taking him out.

With a new target to assassinate, Cristal immediately started making arrangements to travel back to New York. It was always a risk being so close to her old home, knowing that old foes still existed and that there were places in the city that could trigger her crippling panic attacks.

But she never failed to fulfill a contract. She was considered one of the best, and with no life, no family, she was dedicated to completing each job.

What would be her ruse while in New York? What name would she go by? Would she fly or take the train?

She immediately disposed of anything connecting her to the agency the proper way—burning it.

Afterwards, she undressed and donned a long, comfortable T-shirt, popped a few small pills into her mouth, and made herself a quick cocktail to relax her as the hot day progressively moved into a balmy evening.

She pushed opened the French doors from the master bedroom suite to a balcony. Barefoot, Cristal stepped onto the balcony and took in a picturesque view of a sprawling Boston from her eighth-floor apartment. There was a large billboard situated on a slant to the east of her home, soaring into the sky, perfectly placed to block the sun's rays. The newest advertisement pictured a kindly old woman, enthusiastically spreading honey on her new fat-free pancakes. Deep-slit wrinkles marked the corner of her mouth down to her chin, and she looked like a ventriloquist's dummy. Past the billboard was a stunning view of Charles River Basin and the beautiful skyline of Boston.

She took a seat in the three-piece loveseat cushion set. The sky was a vast blue, clear and looked so peaceful.

Her new agency, GHOST Protocol (Gather Humans Only to Slaughter Them) was a rival to her old one, the Commission. It was an eerie acronym, but the company had been very beneficial to her. She had gotten rich off other people's miseries, and murders. However, money wasn't everything; revenge was sweeter.

GHOST Protocol had a lot of similarities with the Commission, but there were differences. She was allowed to have a family, but at her own risk. If a husband, kids, mother, sister, uncle, or whoever found out what she did for a living, and if the agency's cover was exposed, then it was instant death for them. No matter who it was.

Another benefit of being with GHOST Protocol was the money. Her services didn't come cheap. It was a good feeling that she was actually able to spend her blood money without any restrictions, unlike working for the Commission. It was directly deposited into a secured account twenty-four hours after the hit. There was no more waiting until she was twenty-five years old to age out. Aging out didn't exist in her new agency. She was able to retire whenever, so they said, with no strings attached.

Nine months after she was left for dead in New York, GHOST Protocol found her. She had been tucked away in witness protection while the government built a phantom case against drug kingpins connected to the dead hit men Tamar killed right after slaughtering her entire family.

Cristal was just biding her time under the government's protection. She was deemed important. She was a miracle, lucky to survive the gruesome hit on her and her family. She needed rehabilitation and a safe haven to get her mind right.

Via the Internet, she was able to locate a hub in D.C. for GHOST Protocol disguised as a mom-and-pop shop type of organization that sold office supplies. She was vetted, recruited, and given a low-key identity, and had been working for them ever since.

Her new home didn't share her existence with any competing agencies, and as far as the Commission was concerned, she had died on her grandmother's floor a few years back with two bullets in her head.

EIGHT

●●●●●●●●●●●●●●●●●●●●●●●●●●●●●●●●●●●●

Suspect running north on Commonwealth Avenue,"
Sharon shouted into her police radio as she chased a
dangerous robbery suspect through the Bronx in the peak
of the late-evening rush hour.

She ran at full speed, her eyes fixed on the man's
tattooed back. He was clad in a wife-beater and cargo
shorts. He was tall and thin, but fast. Her arms rapidly
went up and down, and her legs moved like a track star's
as she breathed hard and sweated profusely in the hot
sun, swiftly moving and dodging the people in her way
on the sidewalk. She was determined to catch the suspect,
Richard Jefferson, who had a warrant out for his arrest
for robbery, attempted murder, and assault. He had been
a menace to society since he was a young teen, and now,
in his late twenties, he showed no signs of slowing down.

The NYPD wanted Richard Jefferson badly. His
picture had been posted on the walls and shown during
roll call in the local NYPD precincts. His latest crime was
robbing a seventy-year-old grandmother at gunpoint as
she entered the lobby of her building after 10 p.m. He

brutally pistol-whipped her and stole a measly thirty dollars from her purse, and she was now in critical condition at Jacobi Medical Center.

While riding with her partner, Brian Mauldin, they came across Richard as he was exiting a corner bodega. Sharon instantly recognized him from the photos posted of him. Brian pulled their unmarked car to the curb. She quickly opened the passenger door with her eyes fixed on their suspect. She was about twenty feet from him when she asked for identification. Richard abruptly turned and ran north on Commonwealth Avenue, and she didn't hesitate to chase after him, her partner trying to pursue in the car.

Sharon was right behind him, not giving up. It was her second foot pursuit since joining the force.

Richard made a hard left on the next corner, rounding the corner perfectly and sprinting like he was Usain Bolt. He didn't falter once. He didn't anticipate Sharon being just as fast. She yelled multiple times for him to stop as he crossed Randall Avenue. He ran into traffic and barely missed getting hit by a box truck.

He continued running. He rolled under a four-foot chain-link fence between two parking lots, and then went across another busy street, doing jumps and zigzagging in his bid to escape.

Sharon was in great shape, though. Where he went, she chased with conviction. Backup hadn't arrived yet, leaving her alone with a dangerous, and possibly armed, suspect. Her adrenaline was running. Dodging traffic with her sidearm in hand, she was ready for a quick takedown. She put a little more pep into her long strides.

Looming ahead of them both was Soundview Houses. Soundview was a decent-size area, lots of apartments, lots of places for Richard to run and hide. She knew that once her suspect entered into the projects, there was no telling where he could hide.

"Stop!" she yelled at the top of her lungs.

He refused to stop.

It would have been easy to shoot, disabling him, but the outcome of another black male being shot, especially in the back, and unarmed, would create a big outcry from the public, and the incident wouldn't look good going into her jacket. So she was about to do things the hard way.

Richard leaped over the small wrought-iron fence leading into the projects. He cut right, and as he did so, he stumbled a little, but never lost his footing. Sharon followed him, leaping too and not stumbling. She was shortening the distance between them. The chase caught attention, and people stood by, transfixed at the action.

Richard sprinted across an open grassy field, and when he looked over his shoulder, he saw Sharon gaining on him. He bolted through a small playground, and without looking, smashed into a parent and small child in a head-on collision, tumbling over them and falling face-first into the sand.

The mother and son shrieked.

For a second, Richard was dazed, but he quickly came to. Seeing his arrest becoming imminent, out came the four-inch folding knife, the handle gripped in his hand. The wild look in his eyes told Sharon he was about to do something really stupid.

She hurried their way. The child and mother were within his hazardous reach. "Don't do it!" she shouted.

Richard lunged for the boy, ready to take him hostage. His mother was ten feet away, her eyes wide with fear for her three-year-old son.

"No! No! Leave my son alone!" she screamed.

As Richard charged at the young boy, Sharon raised her sidearm and aimed. It was all happening too fast. She saw the boy's life in danger. Richard was a known felon, violent, unpredictable, and once he had that little boy gripped in his arms, there was no telling what he might do.

Police sirens could be heard blaring in the distance. Help was coming fast. But there was no time to wait for help. She had to make a choice. So before Richard fully could grasp the young boy, she planted her feet in the dirt with her arms outstretched, her sidearm steady in her grip and fired.

Boom!

Richard jerked backwards and spun, the bullet ripping through the right side of his chest. He fell over and landed on his side.

Was he dead or alive? She didn't know. She ran over, her gun still drawn and glared at the suspect. Quickly, the mother ran to her child and snatched him up into her comforting arms, her face awash with tears and relief at the same time.

Richard Jefferson was dead.

It was Sharon's first police shooting. Her heart was beating so fast, it felt like it was about to jump out of her chest.

Seconds later half a dozen uniformed police officers converged on the projects with their guns drawn. Sharon was standing over the suspect, knowing this incident had thrust her into a whirlwind of craziness.

There was an on-scene investigation.

The most critical investigation in any law enforcement agency is that of an officer-involved shooting. Shootings like the one Sharon had experienced brought media attention, citizen inquiries, liability issues, and, if handled incorrectly, irreparable damage to the department's reputation.

The first question would be, "Was the shooting justifiable?"

The on-scene investigation included all aspects of a serious crime scene investigation, as well as additional videotaping of the scene and the onlookers.

The lieutenants and captain came out to inspect the scene themselves, talk to Sharon, and come up with their own conclusion.

The media didn't delay in covering the deadly shooting. The police commissioner came also. It became a circus, and Sharon felt like the clown, the center of attention.

With all the pandemonium happening around her, her cell phone rang. The number on the caller ID was unfamiliar to her. She didn't want to answer at the moment with so much going on around her, but she did anyway.

The voice on the other end was a surprise. "I heard you've been looking for me," it said. It was Tamar.

Now she calls, Sharon thought.

•••

It had been almost two weeks since Sharon's involvement in the deadly shooting. Many proclaimed her a hero for saving a three-year-old's life. The incident made the front page of every newspaper in the city with her picture posted. But while some praised her, there were others criticizing her, only seeing another young black male shot dead by a gung-ho police officer, despite the fact that weeks earlier, the man, with a violent rap sheet as long as his arm, had brutally beat an elderly woman and put her in the hospital.

There was a lot of red tape involved, and Sharon only wanted to do her job. Now, she had her own story to tell and was worried about repercussions for trying to do her job. The force placed her on light duty until the investigation came to a conclusion.

Sharon climbed out of her Fiat and gazed at Lindenwood Diner on Linden Boulevard. The place looked retro, but it had some of the best food around. It was early afternoon, and the diner was semi-crowded with a lunch crowd. The parking lot was filling up with cars fast. Sharon walked toward the restaurant dressed in jeans, a

T-shirt, and sneakers, her gun and badge concealed.

Inside the somewhat known diner, the atmosphere was nice, not overcrowded, with soft lighting at the tables and a good wine list, as well as fantastic food and service.

Sharon looked around and spotted Tamar already seated at a booth near the rear. She'd come like Sharon had asked. There was no smile, only concerns and questions for Tamar. The closer Sharon approached, the more she took in Tamar's upgraded appearance. Her legs were crossed, with the right leg wagging over the other, like she was edgy about something. Sharon noticed her jewelry—diamond earrings drooping from her ears, with a diamond bracelet and necklace to match. Tamar's striking beauty caught the attention of a few men nearby.

Tamar's attention was on the newspaper in front of her, a section open with the headline about Sharon. Tamar already had her drink beside her, hot coffee. She hadn't ordered yet. Tamar lifted her eyes from the newspaper and stared at Sharon. She didn't smile either.

"It's been a long time, Sharon," Tamar said.

"I know."

Sharon slid into the booth and sat opposite her. They had grown up together, but today, they felt like strangers as they sat uncomfortably. They had both changed. It showed right away.

Sharon was an honest cop, dedicated and committed to making a change in her community, while Tamar had become darker than her usual self, and cold, developing into a megalomaniac.

"I see you're famous," Tamar said. She motioned with her index finger toward Sharon's picture in the newspaper, tapping her manicured fingernail on her black-and-white photo. "How does it feel to become a killer?"

Sharon took offense. "That's not funny, Tamar," she said. "That's someone's life gone."

"For good reason, I assumed. You're a hero in everyone's eyes. You should celebrate."

"I was only doing my job."

"Still goody two-shoes and lame like always."

"And what have you become?"

"Me? Better." Tamar smirked. "But how did it feel when you took that man's life?" Tamar was like a journalist, eager to know the details, desperate to creep inside Sharon's head and test her character.

Tamar always wondered if Sharon had gone with them that day to Long Island, stepped into the church with them, if the Farm would have changed her too. She had refused, assumed the opportunity bogus, and had also found love with Pike. Tamar always danced around the "what if" with Sharon. Would she have survived the process?

"I think about it every day and night since it happened," Sharon said about the shooting.

"I bet you do."

Tamar looked at Sharon with little admiration. Cop or not, Sharon was beneath her now. She was someone subpar, not to be taken seriously, and she'd been trying to belittle her since the moment she'd sat down across from her.

Sharon knew Tamar was into something illegal. The fancy wardrobe, the jewelry, and in the parking lot of the diner, she noticed a black BMW 650i parked. It didn't take a rocket scientist to figure out the car belonged to Tamar, especially with BMW keys on the table next to her. Sharon speculated that whatever Tamar was into, Cristal was into the same thing. The both of them were two peas in a pod, and it was probably the reason Cristal was murdered.

"Do you miss them?" Sharon asked.

"Who? Cristal and Mona? Yes. Every single day I think about them and wish it was different."

"Different?" Sharon raised her eyebrow. "Different how?"

"You know what I mean."

"I don't, Tamar. Please elaborate for me. What got Cristal killed?"

"Her foolishness," Tamar answered straightforwardly.

"And Mona?"

"I'm sorry about what happened to Mona. When I heard about both their deaths, it fucked me up for a long time. I couldn't sleep. I couldn't eat."

Tamar feigned sympathy for her two friends, but Sharon wasn't buying it. Tamar knew more about their murders than she was telling. The look in her eyes was very unsettling. Sharon just couldn't put her finger on it.

"What got her killed?" Sharon asked again.

"Sharon, you always been a smart girl. Think. Cristal was into all kinds of shit, and loving those type of niggas—drug dealers and bad boys."

"And you weren't, Tamar?"

"Yes, I was, but you knew she had it bad. Her last boyfriend, Hugo, he was a train wreck waiting to happen. It was drug-related. From what I heard, they found cocaine all over that apartment. She had changed, Sharon. In fact, I'm shocked Cristal allowed her grandmother's apartment to turn into a drug den and get all those people murdered."

Sharon was shocked that Tamar was throwing Cristal under the bus so easily. They all had their flaws growing up, and none of them were angels. In reality, all her friends had done things to survive the streets and put food on the table. But she couldn't believe Cristal would jeopardize her grandmother Hattie's safety and that of her other family members so foolishly. She was smarter than that. Cristal loved her family, especially her grandmother. And why was Tamar suddenly speaking so disdainfully about her best friend? It all didn't add up.

"Hello, ladies. How are y'all today? I'm Cynthia. Can I take your drink orders?" the waitress said with a warm smile, interrupting their talk.

Tamar told her, "I'm fine with coffee."

"I'll have some water."

The waitress continued to smile, taking down their drink orders. She passed Sharon a menu, but Sharon didn't have much of an appetite.

When the waitress was out of earshot, Sharon asked, "And what about Mona? Why was she murdered? Was she into some grimy shit too?"

"You're barking up the wrong tree with questions, Sharon," Tamar replied, sounding a little uptight. "I'm nobody's keeper. Everyone was a grown-ass woman, making their own decisions, and they didn't need me always in their business. I had my own shit going on, especially with my mama."

The waiter came over with Sharon's glass of water and another coffee for Tamar.

"Would you like to order now, ladies?" she asked politely.

"Just a salad for me," Sharon said.

Tamar waved her hand indifferently, indicating she didn't want anything else.

"Okay, ladies, I'll be right back."

The minute the waitress was away from their booth, Sharon locked eyes with Tamar. "Why didn't you come to their funerals?"

"I couldn't see my friends like that," she lied.

"You were their friend. It would have been the right thing to do. And I honestly feel if anybody knows why Cristal and Mona were murdered, it should be you. You and Cristal were very close."

"It doesn't mean a damn thing," Tamar spat.

The rift between them was growing wider. Tamar started to get defensive. Sharon was a cop, so it was in her mind to interrogate someone. The Farm had trained Tamar, and the Academy had trained Sharon.

When Sharon's salad was placed in front of her, the talk somehow drifted to the topic of Pike. Tamar wanted to know if the cops had reopened the investigation about his unsolved murder. Sharon lied and said to her, "It was never closed."

Sharon didn't know why she lied to Tamar, but she did. She was personally trying to investigate his case and bring about justice. She believed that one day his killers would be found, tried, convicted, and sent to a lengthy sentence. She wanted to meet Pike's killer or killers face to face, not knowing his killer was seated directly in front of her, feigning innocence about everything that went on.

"I really liked Pike. I knew y'all two would have made a happy couple."

"I think about him every single day." A moment of sadness overcame Sharon, thinking about her loss.

"What kind of gun was he killed with again?" Tamar casually sipped her coffee. She knew the question would taunt Sharon.

"Does it matter?" Sharon retorted.

"It doesn't. Just talking and asking a question."

"Why would you ask me that, anyway?"

"Don't take it personal, Sharon. Pike was my friend too. And he is missed. I hope they do find his killers."

"I hope so too, because whoever killed him will pay for it. I promise, they will. There will be justice."

"I know there will be, and with you being a cop now, I guess you're going to become part of that justice, huh?"

"Damn right, I am."

Tamar smiled. "Keep hope alive. Just remember, they still haven't found who shot Tupac."

Is she with or against me?

Tamar was trying to bark on Sharon, but Sharon wasn't having it. She wasn't a punk, and Tamar wasn't either. They both thought they could take each other if things escalated between them.

As Sharon took a few bites of her salad, she had a few questions to ask Tamar. There was one thing that had always bothered her.

"You know, ever since the four of y'all went to Long Island to do that interview, things were never the same," Sharon said. "Right around the time y'all returned was when Pike was killed, and Lisa never returned with y'all at all."

"What are you implying, Sharon?"

"What really went on there? I don't believe Lisa ran off with some man and left her good home and loving parents. If I remember correctly, everything fell apart and got strange right after Pike took us to that party and E.P. came into the picture. How could so many friends in one crew get murdered or go missing?"

Tamar remained nonchalant. "Proves what you know, Sharon. I've heard from Lisa throughout the years."

Sharon raised her eyebrow. "You have?"

"Yes."

"So where is she?"

"She's happy. Brooklyn, it was draining her dry."

"So you're the only one she's contacted in the past few years?"

"And why wouldn't she?"

Sharon knew Tamar was lying through her teeth. Nothing she was saying fit Lisa's profile. She knew Lisa would never leave without letting her parents or her friends know where she was. Sharon and Lisa were close, like Cristal and Tamar were close, and she wouldn't just run off with some man and not be heard from years later. Everything Tamar was saying was causing more questions to form in Sharon's mind.

Tamar pushed her coffee aside. She was finished talking to Sharon. "Look, it's been an interesting reunion between us, but I have things to take care of. It's been cute." Tamar smirked. She began gathering her things. Before leaving, she went into her purse and dropped a hundred-dollar bill onto the table. "The meal's on me, plus the tip," she said with a smug look. "Let's keep in touch."

And leaving a hundred-dollar bill on the table for a meal that only cost ten dollars was a quite a statement from Tamar. She was saying something to Sharon loud and clear.

Sharon simply stared at Tamar, as she sashayed from the table toward the exit, catching some attention from other diner patrons. Sharon didn't know what to say. She got up herself and left.

The second Sharon walked out of the diner, she noticed Tamar getting into the 650i. She was dead on.

Tamar started the car, backed out of her parking spot, and rolled the window down. Slowly driving by, she waved at Sharon, showing off.

NINE

•••••••••••••••••••••••••••••••••••••

Cristal sat in the public park enjoying her moment of solitude. It was a gorgeous day with an attractive, cloudless blue sky above the city of Boston. The green grass was blowing gently in the summer breeze on the beautiful strip of green that ran beside the Charles River Basin.

A gentle breeze blew through her hair as she sat on a park bench beneath a shade tree a slight distance from the other park-goers. She watched a dog running to catch a Frisbee from his owner, and then a ball. Kids were laughing and playing, and a few joggers were repeatedly circling the area, trying to keep themselves in shape. She looked up to observe squirrels chasing each other up and down the tree. The moment was picturesque.

She was alone and thinking. She'd received the murdergram the day before, and already she knew everything there was to know about her target, Chow Ling Tao—his family, his kids, his habits, his flaws, his likes, and his addiction. In a few hours, she would be on the red eye to JFK Airport. From there, she planned on meeting with her handler, someone who would provide her with the toys she needed to do her job.

She spent another hour lingering in the park, keeping to herself, wishing her life had turned out differently. But harboring regrets about her past would only stir up emotions that she couldn't afford to have. Being nostalgic could not only affect her job; it could get her killed.

She stood up and walked away. The sun was gradually fading behind the horizon. The day at the park was soon about to become a memory. She needed to go home and finish packing.

•••

She walked into her apartment and went straight for her desktop. She powered it on and sunk her bottom into the black task chair and focused on the screen. Microsoft Word came up. She was working on another book—a bonus edition. So far, three chapters revealed what went down at her grandmother's place. The words poured out, the horror she felt, the betrayal, her anger and her survival. It was hard to write, but it gave her an escape.

She quickly wrote a chapter about Hugo, her fingertips rapidly drumming against the keyboard, bringing thought to life. She wished she could bring other things to life. The words came out of her like a torrent.

Two hours later, two more chapters had been completed. She felt proud. The words on the screen were so real to her, it made her suddenly get up and walk out onto her balcony for some fresh air.

•••

The American Airlines flight's wheels came screeching down on the tarmac at JFK Airport. The red-eye flight had just landed in the pre-dawn hour, and over a dozen passengers were ready to exit from the plane. The city was gradually coming alive. Terminal 8 wasn't congested with departing and arriving passengers yet. It was still in slumber for the moment.

Cristal strode off the plane with her carry-on in hand, moving quickly toward the exit of the terminal. For her, the red-eye flight was the best: less people, less traffic, and she wasn't aggravated by the late-night travel. She didn't suffer from fatigue, but was cool and ready to handle her business.

She strutted through the terminal and outside, where cabs waited to pick up passengers. Cristal remained low key, looking casual and unassuming, wearing a pair of jeans, flats, a fedora hat, and huge shades. She hurried toward the nearest cab and jumped inside.

"Welcome to New York," the Hispanic driver greeted, smiling and looking animated. "And where are we headed today?" He glanced at Cristal through his rearview mirror.

The fedora she wore was pulled low over her brow, and she looked like a shadow in the backseat. "Manhattan. Waldorf Astoria on Park Avenue."

"Manhattan it is," he said.

What is he so happy about?

Traffic outside the arrival terminal was sparse. A little over two dozen passengers were on the curb with their luggage and waiting to head toward their destination in the city.

"First time in New York?" he asked.

"No," she replied, being short with him.

She remained distant as the yellow cab navigated through the intricate roadways of the airport. JFK Airport was a labyrinth of overpasses and winding highways leading in and out of Queens. Cristal sat back into the backseat, staring aimlessly outside the window.

Cristal had never been too familiar with Queens. Brooklyn and Harlem were always the preferred places to be and hang out while she was growing up. She'd always thought that Queens was a corny borough, filled with houses and parks; it was the suburbs she could never relate to while growing up in and around the projects.

While on the northbound Van Wyck Expressway, her mind drifted toward Sharon. In Boston, before boarding her plane, she'd seen Sharon's picture in *The Boston Globe* with the caption, "New York Cop Considered a Hero."

Sharon a police officer. Who would have thought? They had been good friends growing up. Like hers, Sharon's life had changed dramatically. Years ago, neither of them would have even thought about becoming a cop or a paid murderer. They once lived normal lives doing teenage things and having teenage problems. They were into the boys, especially the bad boys, and committing illegal acts to come up in their neighborhood.

Cristal didn't have any beef with Sharon becoming a police officer. In fact, she was proud of her. With what she had been through, her friend deserved some happiness in her life. Sharon was the only one who'd made it out of the ghetto unharmed, despite witnessing her boyfriend's murder. She and Tamar had taken away the best thing Sharon had in her life, Pike. They were obviously in love, but because of choices that were made, offing Pike was unavoidable.

The cab went through the Midtown Tunnel and emerged into midtown Manhattan. The early hour made the traffic tolerable. The cab continued to head west, toward the Waldorf Astoria.

When the cab pulled up to the luxury hotel on Park Avenue, Cristal already had his fare in hand. She passed him a hundred-dollar bill and said, "Keep the change."

"Wow! Thank you, miss," he said joyously.

She couldn't help but smile for a fleeting second as she removed herself from the cab and walked toward the hotel. At six a.m., the Waldorf wasn't yet completely alive with activity. She sauntered into the grand lobby with the giant crystal chandelier and marble flooring amid the architectural grandeur and sophisticated style.

She went to the front desk to check in. She looked like a tourist in the city for personal reasons, but it was business. Her target was staying there so she wanted to be close. Lincoln Center wasn't far from the hotel.

She walked into her hotel room, which featured an oversized marble bathroom, and gazed out the window from the tenth floor. It felt good to be back in the city again. She had missed it.

Now that Cristal was there, it was time to put her skills to use. Taking someone's life for profit had become the norm for her a long time ago. She never lost any sleep over the people she had killed through the years. It had her thinking, *Why was I born to do this?*

•••

Being back in New York for the moment and having some time to spare, Cristal took some free time for herself. She took a taxicab to a place to the last place she expected to be. She had no idea why she'd come, but she was there, standing in front of Pike's grave. He was her first kill outside of the Farm. He was her friend, but yet, for advancement in their coldblooded careers, she and Tamar had taken him out like he was a bug on the concrete. She stared at his headstone and remembered the good times they had together as friends. At one point, Cristal liked him and wanted to fuck him, but Sharon beat her to the punch. She had been happy for her friend.

So much had changed since that summer. But now wasn't a time to reflect on the past. The past was dead to her, and all of her friends, Mona and Lisa, were dead too. Sharon was living a new life, and Tamar, though she was still alive, the bitch was dead to her. Cristal wanted that meaning to become literal.

She crouched lower to Pike's grave and exhaled. The summer sun was bearing down on her, and the environment was tranquil. "I'm sorry," she said quietly. "It was a job, and you truly didn't deserve this." Thinking back was painful, so she tried not to do it. She didn't shed any tears. Her well had dried a long time ago. Each passing day seemed like it was harder than the next, but she carried on.

Cristal rose to her feet and turned, making her exit from the cemetery. She climbed back into the idling cab waiting for her outside the gates of the cemetery. She sat back and told the driver, "Take me back to the city."

He nodded, put the cab into drive, and drove off slowly.

While riding in the backseat, she closed her eyes and drifted off to a place before the turbulence and the bloodshed. She popped a few pills into her mouth without any chaser. With her eyes closed, the window down, and the cool breeze blowing against her, she tried to cure her issues. The medication was a temporary relief.

The stress of another contract to fulfill wasn't much of a burden; the more bodies, the easier the killing became. It only took patience and cunning movements to become a devious contract killer. She couldn't afford to make any mistakes, so every movement she made was well planned. A Chinese diplomat would be one of her most difficult assignments. Chow Ling Tao was a popular and wealthy man with a lot of enemies. He walked around with security, with all of his movements recorded and watched. It was going to take someone with balls, great tactical skills, wits, and patience to take him out. Cristal was all of the above.

She was in the man's head, already knowing his routine and his schedule. She had hacked into his computer, observed him and his security detail from afar, and studied his favorite places to eat while visiting the city. Now, all that was left was when and where to strike with the least risk.

She had assessed different locations, from the Waldorf to Lincoln Center, and tried to determine which site in Manhattan would be most conducive to a long-range assassination.

Earlier, she had gone to see her handler—Mr. Zero was what they called him—at an undisclosed location in New Jersey. The handler worked various locations throughout the nation. He was something like a moving parts store, except that he moved deadly weapons, from handguns and grenades to long-range sniper rifles and bombs.

Mr. Zero pulled up in his black old-school Lincoln Continental and stepped out, pulling on a cigarette and looking harder than any man Cristal had ever known. He was an older Italian man who moved with confidence. His face was blunt, with harsh features, like he'd been chipped from rock and all the rough edges left untouched. The lines in his pale face looked like wrinkled paper, and his eyes were colder than the Arctic and exhibited a man who been there and done that—a retired stone-cold killer. He was of average height, stocky, and dressed in nondescript dark pants and a dark jacket, the gray in his cropped hair a testament to his age.

With his keys in his hand, he opened the trunk to reveal the goodies he had for Cristal. The trunk of the Continental was filled with guns, guns, and more guns. While standing by the trunk, smoking his cigarette, Mr. Zero eyed Cristal from head to toe and said, "Take your time, and let the weapon pick you."

Cristal nodded.

She opted to go with a Blaser R93 LRS2 sniper rifle. It had to be assembled, but that wasn't a problem for Cristal. She removed it from his trunk and placed it into a briefcase.

Mr. Zero nodded. "Great choice." He closed his trunk, walked toward the driver's side, and climbed into his car.

The deed was done. No more words were exchanged between them.

Cristal walked the opposite way with the briefcase in hand. Now that she had the weapon, it was time to make headlines.

For the next two days, Cristal acted like she was a tourist and went sight-seeing to kill some time. She visited Times Square, walked through Central Park, went up to the top of the Empire State Building, and wined and dined herself in some lovely restaurants. It was her job to act unassuming, and she did a very good job at it. Regardless of the troubles and demons plaguing her mind, she pulled off being the perfect easygoing character. No one would've suspected she was in town for something sinister.

TEN

●●●●●●●●●●●●●●●●●●●●●●●●●●●●●●●●●

The clear day, with a warm sun pitched high in the sky, looked like a postcard moment. Tamar found herself engrossed in Melissa Chin's new book as she sat butt-naked on her balcony. She became infuriated reading through the remaining pages of the latest novel. It was all there, their story, from beginning to end, but it was being told as fiction. It read like a Donald Goines novel, well written and detailed. Laced within the pages were the exploits of her former crew, once known as the Cristal Clique. Tandi and Olivia, two characters in the book, obviously represented herself and Cristal, the difference being the characters all grew up in Harlem, while Tamar and Cristal had grown up in Brooklyn. Tamar was reading the same events they went through with only the names and locations changed.

In Melissa Chin's first book, it was all about boosting, sex, stealing, fighting, and growing up rough in the jaws of Harlem, trying not to be swallowed and forgotten. The writer was way too familiar with Tamar and her friends' lives. In one chapter of the book, one secret was spilled that only Tamar, Cristal, and Mona knew about.

Tandi and I came up with the plan to rob the Chinese man late that evening, and Sarah had no choice but to go along with it. We were hungry like an African village, and with only three dollars between the three of us, we decided to commit our first wicked act. The deliveryman seemed like an easy mark. We would always see him delivering for Great Wall throughout our hood on his colorful moped with his own ghetto pass to come through untouched because niggas were always hungry. Tandi made the call. Sarah and I were nervous, but ready to go through with it. We were fifteen years old, bored, hungry, and broke, and we wanted to have some fun and feed our stomachs at the same time.

After placing the order, the only thing left to do was to wait. Forty minutes later, there was a knock at the apartment door. It wasn't our place; we weren't stupid enough to give him our real address. The apartment we occupied that evening was a former crack den that had been vacant for weeks. Police had raided it a few weeks back, arrested everybody, and didn't secure it well enough. So, we took advantage of the place. We had sex and sucked dick there, smoked weed, drank, joked around, and loitered in the apartment, making it our own ghetto haven.

Tandi was always the wildest and most promiscuous one out of all of us. With the delivery man knocking, waiting to make his delivery, she looked at me and Sarah, and said, "Watch how I get this nigga's attention."

Unexpectedly, she stripped down to her panties and bra and went to answer the door raw like that. That was Tandi, unpredictable and crazy to do anything for attention. She opened the door, and once that China deliveryman caught a good look at the fifteen-year-old showing off her curves, ample breasts, and brown skin, he was utterly shocked.

"You got my food, right?" Tandi said, smiling at him.

He nodded. "*Twen-tee fif-tee*," he said.

"Okay, let me get the money." She pivoted and walked away, luring him deeper into the apartment.

Once he stepped foot inside, I hit him in the back of the head with a brick from outside. I didn't think I had hit him that hard, but he tumbled over like a tree, falling face-first against the dusty floor. I saw blood and panicked. He wasn't moving at all.

"Oh shit!" Sarah uttered, looking wide-eyed and scared.

"Yo, get the food!" Tandi said.

Sarah quickly snatched the plastic bag of food from the floor.

Tandi had another brainstorm. She was ready to knock out two birds with one stone. "Yo, go through his pockets. I know this nigga got money in them."

I went through his pockets and removed ninety-five dollars. I was so nervous, I could feel my heart trying to beat through my chest. It sounded like the loudest thing in the room.

"He dead?" Sarah asked.

"Nah," Tandi said, dressing quickly. "Olivia just fucked him up, but he ain't dead."

We rushed from that apartment like it was on fire and about to disintegrate. We had our food and some spending cash. As we were trying to ease all of our nerves and forget about what we'd done, we filled our stomachs with free food and got high from two blunts. The next day we went shopping on Pitkin Avenue.

Tamar clenched her fist, her blood boiling. After reading that chapter about her life from years ago, she wanted to tear the pages from the book and burn them, but there were plenty more books where that came from. She remembered that night so vividly in her head. The man wasn't dead, but Cristal had really fucked him up. It was on the news that he had to be taken to the hospital and received seventeen stitches in the back of his head. Subsequently, he'd suffered some brain damage.

But they'd never told anyone about that incident. They had all gotten away with it. Detectives did a thorough investigation, but never came sniffing the girls' way. The call was made from a public payphone, and the address was a vacant apartment commonly used by everyone living in the projects. So who was snitching suddenly? Both Cristal and Mona were dead . . . unless Mona told someone before her death.

In Melissa Chin's second novel, she wrote about when they were seventeen and a friend of theirs was murdered brutally:

I can remember standing on the Harlem corner with Tandi and Sarah one summer afternoon, when suddenly cop cars came flying by us with their lights blaring. They came to an abrupt stop in the vacant parking lot. A body had been found in the dumpster. The word had gotten out that it was a young girl our age, dead. She was naked, brutally beaten, raped and thrown out like she was yesterday's trash.

We were all taken aback by the news, but we were even more taken aback when we found out the identity of the girl. Her name was Shakiyla Davis. We went to school together, and she lived around the corner from me. I couldn't hold back my tears after hearing about what happened to her, Sarah too. But Tandi remained aloof and showed no empathy at all.

That day, I saw something in Tandi, something sinister, like she could be a serial killer in the making. What I saw in her didn't scare me, but it intrigued me. Death didn't seem to bother her; in fact, I think she was fascinated by it. Was I too? We were all subversive creatures from the ghetto, trying to find our way, trying to survive somehow, some way.

It didn't take long for Shakiyla's mother to hear about her daughter's gruesome death, and she came running from her apartment in an undignified haste. The tears had already started brewing in her eyes, panic on her face; it was a look that I will never forget. When she reached the crime scene, her daughter's body had already been removed from the foul-smelling dumpster and covered with a white sheet. She collapsed in the arms of her neighbor, falling to her knees in grief. She shrieked and cried so loud, her wail pierced all of Brooklyn that afternoon.

Tamar continued reading the second book. It was only the beginning of more secrets, lies, motives, and murders that were never to be told again being revealed through works of fiction. One chapter was particularly worrisome to Tamar. It delved into the details of the Commission, but was renamed the Syndicate in the trilogy.

The third book was the one E.P. had left on her bed. This one was the biscuits and gravy of the trilogy. The drama between Tandi, Olivia, and Sarah escalated. Supposedly, it was the last book, but at the end, it hinted at another book being written.

The area in Texas was a hamlet and census-designated place, almost on the tip of Texas in the town of Galveston. White people were everywhere, smiling, looking jolly like Santa Claus, and hurrying to their purpose of the day. We all felt like fish out of water, everything being strange and new to us.

The instructions given to me once we arrived in town were to go to a Baptist church located five miles from the railroad station. There wasn't any pickup service for us. We had to find our own way to this church where our lives were supposedly going to change for the better.

We finally arrived at the white-steepled Baptist church on Johnson Avenue in the quiet suburban area with the picketed fences, tree-lined streets, and sprawling green lawns. We had to split the fare between the four of us, a worrisome feeling, since we were on our last dime. Shit, we'd never been outside of New York before, and now we were over a thousand miles away from home in some small Texas country town without a clue what to do next.

The cab driver gazed at me evenly. "Is there a problem here, ladies?"

"Nah, no problem," I returned unworriedly, focusing on the driver.

"You sure there's no problem here?" the driver reiterated evenly.

I told him, "Look, we pay you to drive us around, not to be in our fuckin' business."

Why I had the sudden irritation, I didn't know. I was scared, but didn't want to show it. I was told to come to Texas believing the words of a man I really liked.

The driver laughed out of the blue. He lit a cigarette and fixed his attention on me and my friends.

"You girls need help, I see," the man said.

"We don't need help," I spat.

"You sure about that, Olivia?" he asked.

"How did you know my name?" I exclaimed.

He puffed on his cigarette and breathed out smoke. He looked into the eyes of all of us, a steady calm about him. He wasn't in any rush to answer my question. I wasn't important to him. Like L.T., he had a job to do. He was paid by the Syndicate to subtly observe our behavior upon our arrival in Texas and give a vital report on each and every one of us. Unbeknownst to us, the testing had already started. We were potential recruits, and once recruits arrived into the town, they were watched as if by a hawk. The people watching could be anybody: the cab driver, a sanitation worker, a cop, the conductor, a housewife, or a teenage girl. It didn't matter. The Syndicate employed people of all ethnicities, creeds, and occupations.

I asked sternly again, "How did you know my name?"

"Because, I was paid to know about you," the man replied with nonchalance.

It suddenly dawned on me that he was part of the Syndicate, or hired by them. My heart jumped, my fiery attitude changed suddenly, and I quickly apologized to him for my behavior.

We entered the Baptist church and saw about thirty other people inside, black, white, and Hispanic, mostly young and eager-looking, supposedly new recruits from all over vying to work for the Syndicate.

Everyone in the room stood around looking lost and out of place, until they were told to find a seat in the pews.

An hour after entering the church, conversations going on, and strangers trying to become familiar with each other, a well-dressed but hard-looking white man with a faded teardrop tattoo under his right eye that looked like it was in the process of being removed by laser and a strong German accent came out to greet us.

"Willkommen jeder!" the man said loudly to the crowd in German, which meant "Welcome, everyone."

He had everyone's undivided attention.

He continued, *"Sie haben einen langen Weg von zu hause gereist...für diese grobe chance."* The man gazed heavily into the small gathering of people before him. He stood on the church platform, his strong presence speaking volumes.

Not a soul in the room understood what he had just said. I didn't either. Some didn't even know he had just spoken in German.

With further reading, the new novel, *Killer Dolls*, ventured farther into forbidden territory. Tamar's eyes went wide when she started reading about Pike's character, who in the book was renamed Traven.

One particular part of the book read:

Traven would probably be our easiest target, but yet, our hardest too. It was close to home. He was our friend. I had no idea why he was on the Syndicate's hit list, but for some reason, they wanted him dead. We thought about the aftermath following his death, especially with Sarah. How was she going to take it? She had fallen in love with Traven, and they had a special bond building. She was our close friend, but we couldn't dwell on outcomes. This was business, and we were broke and needed to prove ourselves.

Tandi and I sat parked in a stolen maroon Chevy on the quiet, narrow Brooklyn block and observed Traven exiting his building. He zipped up his jacket in the cool fall air and started to walk down the street alone.

We each wore large black hoodies, dark, baggy jeans, latex gloves, Timberlands, and ski hats, trying to give off the impression we were two black males seated in the car.

I was behind the wheel, the .9mm loaded and cocked back on my lap. Tandi gripped the same caliber of gun. We both were ready to get it over with. Our forty-eight hours to do the hit were winding down. We had devised a plan to make it look gang-related. It was no secret that Traven was a drug dealer and womanizer, so his death could have come from anybody from rival dealers or a jealous boyfriend.

"When you wanna do this?" Tandi asked.

"When he comes back," I said.

"That could be hours."

"He won't be gone long," I returned.

"How you know?"

"I just know."

I knew it wasn't going to be a long wait by what he had on: some sweat pants, sneakers, and a gray hoodie underneath his fall jacket. It looked like he was making a quick run to the corner store.

"Remember, make it look gang-related. We in and we out," I said.

Tandi nodded.

Tamar stood from her chair and tossed the book in a different direction. Filled with frustration and anger, she wanted to scream. There was no reason to read on, since she already knew how it was going to end. How could this be? How could this author have so much information about her and her friends' lives?

The majority of the story was told in detailed first person, though some particulars had been changed slightly. The Dinkins brothers had been fictionalized as the Johnson brothers. One of their earlier assignments, the killing of the groom at his wedding via poison, was written as a baby shower assassination. And the Cristal Clique had been fictionalized as Murder Inc.

Fucking Murder Inc.? It doesn't get any more transparent than that.

Tamar was ready to tear Melissa Chin apart with her bare fucking hands. But, first, she wanted to torture her and find out where she got her information from. What source was feeding her the material? It was killing Tamar to know how the fuck that bitch knew so many intimate details about their operation.

With everyone from the original crew who knew about the Farm dead, she suspected Mona, while residing in the Bronx, had probably run off her mouth to someone. Maybe it had been to a journalist, in confession to a priest, or to an average Joe crafty enough to jot down all her tales and profit from it.

Now Mona was dead, and so was Cristal, and E.P. had confirmed that Lisa had been killed at the Farm. So who?

It hadn't been until the latest novel, *Killer Dolls*, that Tamar finally had a face to go with the name. She studied the bitch's photo intently, scrutinizing every feature, hoping for something to jog her memory. Where did she know this girl from? Did she even know this girl at all? Was she someone from their old neighborhood? A friend of a friend? Maybe, an enemy? Was the bitch somehow overlooked while she was growing up?

Tamar thought hard. She had never seen the girl before. Melissa Chin was young, pretty, and a dead bitch walking. She just didn't know it yet. Whoever said the game should be sold not told needed a foot shoved up their ass.

ELEVEN

★★★★★★★★★★★★★★★★★★★★★★★★★★★★★★★

E.P. and his beautiful acquaintance for the night stepped out of his burgundy Bugatti Veyron 16.4 Super Sport. He had parked in front of a building with dark blue awning protruding from its brightly lit glass doorway on the Upper West Side of Manhattan, 78th Street to be exact. Looking sharp and handsome in his dark charcoal cashmere wool Giorgio Armani suit, he grabbed his date by her slim waist and pulled her closer to him. They both were all smiles and laughter tonight. They had left a special charity event hosted at the Trump Tower, and now, for E.P., the real fun was about to begin. He couldn't wait to have his privacy with Karen, who was model-beautiful, with curves in the right places and an attractive smile that could light up any room. She was something to take his mind away from the problem shaping as the latest Melissa Chin novel had reached #15 on *The New York Times* Best Sellers list.

Karen, clad in a long, shimmery dress that pooled around her high heels, threw herself against E.P.'s shoulder and giggled like a young schoolgirl as they walked arm-in-arm into the bright lobby of the building. They strode through the marble lobby, passing the overnight doorman, looking like a friendly couple, and headed toward the array of elevators waiting to lift them high in the sky to their designated floor. It was after midnight, so with most people asleep, the building was quiet like a cemetery.

The two stepped into E.P.'s lavish penthouse suite on the top floor, and Karen was immediately dazzled by nearly 7,000 square feet of opulence. She removed her high-heeled sandals and walked through the place with them dangling on one finger.

"You live here?" she asked in awe.

"I like the best," he said, "from my home to my women."

She smiled.

He quickly gave her a tour of the place. E.P. didn't mind showing off his wealth. He was a rich man and a playboy, so seducing and sexing beautiful women was his forte.

"This is *beautiful*," Karen said.

"*You're* beautiful."

Karen turned to face him. His handsome face and nice build excited her. Just being close to him stirred up some strong sexual cravings inside of her. Her womanhood was becoming absolutely moist from his touch and his eyes locking into her.

"What do you do again?" she asked, not caring, but making conversation so she wouldn't look like a complete slut yearning for some dick.

"I do a little bit of this, and a little bit of that," he said.

Karen smiled. She couldn't contain the lust bubbling inside of her. She walked closer to the railing of the picturesque terrace to view the illuminated city.

E.P. got behind her, wrapped his arms tightly around her, and held her closely, making sure she felt his growing erection poking her in the back. He then placed his lips against the nape of her neck and landed a few sweet kisses against her skin. He maneuvered his hand into her dress, pulled out her breast, and played with her nipple.

He then pulled up her dress. As his fingers probed deeper, her breathing was getting more labored. She was so wet, E.P.'s fingers were coated with her juices.

She wanted to fuck him right there. She turned to face him again, her dress looking unhinged from her slim, yet curvy, frame.

Things started to get a little more heated, and they started to kiss intensely. She reached below and unzipped his pants. Her hand extended inside, and she grabbed his dick and started stroking him into a full erection, causing him to moan. Pressed against him on the terrace, she could see his eyes roll back in his head as she squeezed his hard shaft and started using both hands in a steady rhythm.

"That feels good." He grabbed her ass and told her not to stop.

His breathing became intense as she rolled his balls around in her fingers.

He was rubbing her clit and biting on her neck. Then he grabbed her shoulders, turned her around, and pushed her against the iron railing. He lifted her dress over her hips and ripped off her panties like they were nothing. E.P. grabbed her hips from behind.

Karen, her nipples against the cold railing, braced herself for penetration.

E.P.'s dick was already out and hard. He slammed it into her in one thrust, and she jerked forward. If she wasn't holding on tight to the railing, he would have pushed her over.

"Ooooh, fuck me!"

She let out a moan like a wounded animal, and it was met with a grunt from him.

She felt his delicious dick sliding in and out of her, hitting her spot, pounding her, and stroking her into a blissful submission. She was backing her ass up on him, which was all she could do to hold on.

E.P. grabbed both her hips and fucked her like a savage.

Her head down, eyes closed, Karen could feel her ass cheeks spreading, with his big dick opening her pussy up like a good book. Her knees were shaking, and all she could feel was pleasure overwhelming her.

Abruptly, he pulled out, stepping back from her and squeezing his dick.

She turned to see what was going on. With his big dick thrusting in and out of her, she couldn't even think straight.

He smirked.

"Why did you stop?" she asked.

E.P. took her by her hand and pulled her toward the bedroom. "Let's continue this inside."

Karen followed his lead, anxious to get things under way again. She had been teased and pleased in ways that were most indescribable.

Both ready to start some fireworks, they pulled their clothes off, leaving a trail all the way to the bed.

In the bedroom, she lay on her back, her wet pussy exposed for him to take again. E.P. climbed on the bed, pushed her legs back, and aimed his cock near her entrance and thrust himself inside. He pistoned himself inside of her, missionary-style. Her legs wrapped around his healthy frame, their bodies entwined into one lustful pretzel.

They were moaning uncontrollably and loudly.

E.P. flipped her over, grabbed her hips, and started working his dick in and out doggy-style, while she buried her face in the pillow to keep her moans of pleasure from having someone call the police.

Karen was chanting an erotic mantra. "Ooooh, fuck me! Fuck me! It feels so good! Harder! Deeper! Harder! I love your big dick in me like this. Fuck me! Yes! Yes!"

With her round ass positioned upward, legs spread, tits plastered against the mattress, and the dick pumping in and out of her, it didn't take long for E.P.'s hot cum to splash on her back.

Then they collapsed on the bed, exhausted and drained.

"I gotta pee," Karen said, lifting herself from the bed and disappearing around the corner to use the bathroom.

E.P. lay on his back, feeling satisfied. He shut his eyes, relishing the moment. The sex was good, and Karen was a fantastic woman.

As he lay naked on his queen-size bed, out of the blue, he thought about Cristal.

How long had it been since her death? As time went by, E.P. missed her greatly. She had been the only woman that had his complete interest, which was a mystery to him. Sanctioning her murder was one of the hardest things he'd had to do.

A minute went by, and then five minutes. When ten minutes passed and Karen didn't come back into the bedroom, E.P. removed himself from the bed, grabbing his .38 that he kept close. Naked and cautious, he walked toward the bathroom, knowing something was wrong. Things felt suddenly still in his penthouse suite. Ten minutes was too long for her to be in the bathroom. He didn't hear any water running, or any movement in the room.

He didn't call out Karen's name, but he gripped the gun tightly and was ready for the unexpected. He slowly rounded the corner with his arm outstretched and the gun aimed toward the bathroom door. It was shut, its white light tipping out under the door into the hallway.

Slowly, he grabbed the doorknob and twisted it, pushing open the bathroom door cautiously and gazing inside. To his surprise, Karen's naked body was sprawled across the white-tiled floor. Her throat had been slashed, and there was a pool of thick crimson blood beneath her.

E.P. remained expressionless. Death wasn't anything new to him. Karen's murder was more surprising than upsetting. He walked farther into the bathroom, disregarding the body. It was evident he had unwanted company in his home.

"I guess this makes us even," a voice chimed from somewhere in the shadows.

E.P. turned and grinned, knowing the voice. "I guess it does."

Tamar loomed from the darkness with a bloody knife in her hand and a cold look about her. Cutting the woman's throat was easy, like slicing butter with a hot knife.

"At least I let you finish."

"I was looking for a second round with her."

"Don't get greedy."

E.P. looked at the bloody knife in her hand. "You bring a knife to a gunfight, I see."

"I brought what I needed."

He chuckled lightly. How had she gotten into his place, past security in the lobby, and through his security code? He hadn't even detected her when he'd arrived home. Maybe he was slipping. Or was she that good? Whatever the reason, the Commission had trained her well.

"And why the reason for this sudden visit?" E.P. asked. "You plan on taking me out too?"

Tamar stepped closer and fixed her eyes on E.P.'s nakedness. His chiseled body was magnificent from head to toe, eye candy all around. His cool manner in dangerous situations was always appealing to her.

"If I wanted you dead, you wouldn't have seen it coming," she said.

He smiled. "I see everything coming."

E.P. tossed his .38 it to the side, feeling confident he didn't have a problem with her.

Tamar didn't move yet, nor did she toss the knife. She didn't feel threatened by him at all. In fact, she was truly in love with him. She was there for business, but his nakedness was distracting.

"I can see something else is on your mind," E.P. said.

"Yes, there is. This Melissa Chin," Tamar spoke evenly.

"Having trouble with the contract?"

"No trouble at all. That bitch will be dead by the end of the week. But one thing is bothering me."

"What's that?"

"Why didn't the Commission place a hit on this bitch when her first book dropped? She knows too much about everything, especially the details about my life. And why so little intel on her? She's a best-selling author. Why is it so hard to locate her? Her business is all over the map."

Usually, the Commission always came correct with names, dates, location, and other private information about the people they wanted dead. With Melissa Chin, they only had a name, which they assumed was a pseudonym. With this target, all E.P. gave her was that same name.

In the beginning, Tamar felt that E.P. was obsessed with murdering Melissa. She wondered why now, after each book dropped, she was the one who felt obsessed to kill the renowned author in a brutal and sadistic way for charting into dangerous territory with her literature.

"Melissa Chin isn't her real name," E.P. said.

"Tell me something I don't know."

"From her picture, we got her prints, and from her prints, we traced her roots back to a small town in Idaho," E.P. said.

"I'm listening."

"She was a druggie. A problem child with occasional outbursts of rage. Her parents went missing a while back—we presume they're dead—maybe she had a hand in their disappearance, and since her last book signing, she's gone missing. She left a note to her fans and friends explaining her sudden absence. We believe someone else is pulling the strings."

"I figured that too. You know who?"

"We don't know yet, but whoever it is, they're good. They've kept themselves hidden. Maybe a ghostwriter. We've gotten word that Melissa Chin's last whereabouts were in Boston. She's back and forth between there and New York." E.P. walked into his bedroom all of a sudden.

Tamar followed.

He pulled open a dresser drawer and removed some papers and tossed them on the bed for her to see.

"MasterCard, American Express, Visa, all credit card applications applied for in her name with the same address in Boston," he said.

Tamar picked up the paperwork and inspected it. "How stupid can this bitch be?"

"Very stupid."

"I'll be in Boston the first thing tomorrow morning," Tamar said. "And I will eradicate the problem and find out who's the real mastermind behind all of this."

E.P. smiled. "That's why you're my number-one bitch."

"Am I?"

"No question about it."

Tamar wanted to believe him.

E.P. threw an engaging look her way. His gaze was intense in her direction, quickly making Tamar lose her focus. Now that business was over, he had the urge to play again, and given that Karen was dead on his bathroom floor with her throat cut, he was hoping Tamar would pick up where she'd left off.

He had always been hard to resist, and Tamar wanted to stay angry with him and leave him completely alone. What they had was a dangerous affair. However, he'd made his intentions clear the last time they saw each other. She wanted to turn from his tempting gaze and walk away, but she didn't know how to quit him. She wished she could, but everything about E.P. was hypnotizing.

"Are you in a rush?" he asked.

She didn't answer him right away. She wanted to fight the urge to have him. As he stood naked in front of her, his lengthy manhood calling out her name, she averted her look from his. No matter how coldblooded a killer she was, she was still a woman, and her feelings were manifested through her behavior. She continually wanted to prove herself to him.

He stepped forward, confident he would have her tonight. "Let's go to bed," he said quietly. He reached out to take her hand, though she still gripped the bloody knife.

Make no mistake about it, Tamar wanted to fuck him, but she always felt used by him. *Did he do Cristal the same way?* she repeatedly asked herself. *Did he love her more than he does me?*

With E.P. standing naked in front of her, she fantasized about all sorts of nasty things. Once she felt his hand touch hers, she dropped the knife to the floor and followed his lead into the bedroom, where he undressed her.

Tamar wanted to be penetrated by him—a beautiful, strong, vicious black man with a deadly past. Like her, he was a killer, and it turned Tamar on so deeply. Thinking about the kills they could amass together was already making her wet and ready to come.

He pushed her against the bed, and she landed on her back, instantly spreading her legs, waiting for his thrust inside of her.

E.P. climbed onto the bed fully erect, ready to take Tamar's body. She didn't care that another woman had just warmed his bed. All that mattered to her was being with him and having him love her back.

The sensation of having his big, black dick rub her pussy lips, teasing her, sliding up and down her slit, made Tamar anxious and excited. He then thrust his thick erection inside of her, making it feel like they became one.

She quickly jerked from his raw entry, grabbing his thick frame tightly, her legs spread for him, feeling his thick, hard dick pound in and out of her, filling her with ecstasy.

"Fuck me!" she cried out.

"Damn, baby! Your pussy feels so fuckin' good."

The pussy had him warped, as her nails dug into his ass cheeks, pulling him deeper and deeper inside her. He fucked her harder and faster in the missionary position.

Tamar could feel herself about to explode soon. There was nothing better than having the full weight of a man on top of her and hearing him speak softly in her ear.

From behind, he fucked her rough and rapid, grabbing her hips. Tamar felt her tits swinging while he thrust repeatedly inside her with all his might, and then, being the freaky nigga he was, he started fingering her asshole.

They both moaned and groaned as he continued to pound her from the back.

Howling, she gripped the headboard, as the bed shook. And then, finally, the explosion she longed for happened. She felt herself coming all over his hard dick from getting thoroughly fucked, tears in her eyes and not knowing what to do with herself.

When it was done, E.P. lifted himself from her petite, sweaty frame, leaving her mashed against the mattress. He smirked. "I gave you what you wanted. Now you give me what I want."

TWELVE

●●●●●●●●●●●●●●●●●●●●●●●●●●●●●●●●●●●●●●●

Lincoln Center for the Performing Arts, the sixteen-acre complex of buildings in the Lincoln Square neighborhood of Manhattan, was teeming with stylish people in the open courtyard. A picturesque fountain flowed during the late summer evening, and the buildings were awash in yellow light. The theater was jumping with the annual fashion/charity fundraiser, and security was tight, with NYPD scattered strategically through the area to protect everyone's well-being.

Chow Ling Tao stepped out of a black Maybach parked not too far from the activity in the square. Flanked by his security detail and his family, he was all smiles, dressed sharply in a black three-button Calvin Klein tuxedo. He grabbed the hands of his two young daughters, ages five and three, and walked toward the Lincoln Center with his wife following. Chow Ling Tao walked and laughed with his two little girls like he didn't have a care in the world.

Four men had set up a small perimeter around him for his and his family's protection. They walked uncontested with their dark suits and earpieces, communicating with each other, their holstered weapons concealed under their jackets. It looked like the president was at the center.

From a short distance, Cristal fixed her eyes on her target. She blended into the crowd easily, disguised as a well-dressed attendee in a long black Versace gown, her scars hidden by a stylish hat and veil. She looked as if she belonged there.

She headed his way, cool and collected. *Keep it simple*, she said to herself.

Chow stopped to chat with a few other attendees before entering the building. He seemed to be a genial man, and far from the dangerous arms dealer and trader of U.S. secrets her organization portrayed him to be. But Cristal knew that looks could be deceiving.

Cristal slowly approached with his bodyguards watching all movement. She pretended to be on her cell phone and abruptly stumbled his way, deliberately falling into him. She hit him with a great force, which immediately sent his security detail into high alert.

"I'm so sorry," she said quickly, looking like an innocent patron of the arts. "I'm just so clumsy."

"Everything's fine. Accidents happen," Chow said, quickly waving off the dogs ready to lunge. "Just a mishap. It appears this young lady is eager to see the show like everyone else," he said, keeping his humor and easygoing attitude intact.

Cristal once again apologized and hurriedly walked away. It was done. It wasn't graceful, but it was effective.

She didn't have to follow behind Chow; she already knew where he was going and his schedule with his family. Her main focus was on the Maybach parked on the street with the driver behind the wheel. She walked closer, looking nonchalant, her attention shrewdly transfixed on the high-end vehicle. She saw something in her favor— The glass wasn't bulletproof, and the exterior of the car wasn't armored. One glimpse of the car and she knew everything about it. Only a trained eye could spot what she spotted.

As the crowd outside slowly but surely walked into the Avery Fisher Hall, home of the New York Philharmonic, Cristal turned and went the opposite way. She calmly crossed Columbus Avenue, where the yellow cabs dominated the city street, and headed toward the towering skyscraper.

Rule number one: Always fit in and never look suspicious—always act like you belong. She effortlessly strolled into the building, gliding through the lobby, and even gave the doorman a slight nod and smile. He smiled back, not seeing anything dubious about the woman in the long gown and makeup. She stepped into the elevator, going to the planned floor, and entered a well-furnished apartment like it was her own.

It belonged to Mr. Schmidt, a German software developer who was out of town for the week on business. She had seen the man in a nearby café, picking him out of a dozen customers after she had overheard his conversation about his impending business trip. She pickpocketed his wallet, gained access to his personal information, and hacked into his email account to find out about his routine and his goings and comings.

His apartment was perfect. It was high enough and positioned precisely to her favor. From the corner window of the living room, she had a direct and flawless 360-degree view of Lincoln Square.

The privileged crowd in the square had withered away into the building, leaving Cristal ample opportunity to get the job done right. She set up near the window, the Blaser R93 LRS2 sniper rifle on the floor and the detachable night scope in her lap. She also had a small Kahr .9mm with six rounds in the magazine. If everything went according to plan, she wouldn't need the .9mm. At this moment, all she had was patience, since the event had only just started.

Cristal didn't move from the small area in the living room. The lavish apartment was dark and completely still. She removed a small device from the clutch she carried and activated the tracker. Unbeknownst to Chow Ling Tao, when Cristal had bumped into him, she'd quickly attached a small tracking device under the lapel of his jacket. Now, she had his exact location inside the theatre and would know his every move.

Two hours went by, and her patience was still strong. Like a statue, she didn't move from the area in the living room. She sat gazing out the window, which was open just wide enough to aim the long, thin barrel of her sniper rifle through.

A small crowd started to trickle from the hall. The show had ended.

Cristal took her position, crouched with one knee on the floor by the window, the sniper rifle gripped expertly in her arms. She glanced at the tracking device indicating Chow's exact location.

The crowd started pouring out heavily from the hall, men and women laughing and chatting. It was hard to see anything from so high and in the dark. Looking for one man in the sea of faces in the night was almost like trying to find Waldo in the crowd, but the device gave her the GPS location of her target.

The Maybach was still parked close by, and the driver was waiting outside for his employer to arrive, ready to open the passenger door for Chow and his family. The Yukon his bodyguards traveled in was parked behind the Maybach.

Cristal had a small open window as Chow approached the vehicle with his family in tow. She could feel the adrenaline sharpening her focus as she raised the rifle to her shoulder and pressed her cheek against the hollowed-out stock. Through the green-and-black night-vision lens, her target's face came clear as he walked calmly with his security detail, looking like he had enjoyed the show.

She took a deep breath. She centered her main targeting chevron over Chow's forehead. When he got within an arm's reach of the door handle, she squeezed off one fast round. The rifle's suppressor allowed a small pop of sound, nothing more.

Chow stiffened for a fraction of a second, the bullet going through his skull. Instantaneously his head lolled to the side, and he collapsed in front of his family and security.

It took a split second before his security detail and family knew something was wrong. Chow collapsed right in front of them, a small hole in his forehead, blood pooling around his head. Instantly, panic and fear gripped the crowd. His wife screamed, and his children were flushed with fright. His security team immediately went into action, crowding around the body with their guns drawn.

Cristal removed herself from the window, dropping the rifle to the ground. It was time to go. She already had an exit plan. She removed a small retro cell phone from her clutch. It was the trigger to a small pipe bomb she had cleverly placed in the stairway of the building she was in. She needed confusion to make her escape easier.

Quickly wiping prints and packing up her toys, she made her way toward the door. The confusion could be heard outside with police sirens blaring, and people yelling and shouting.

She walked out the apartment into the carpeted hallway and hurried toward the service elevator. Descending down into the lobby, before the doors opened, she pressed the call button on her cell phone sending radio waves to set off the device, the cell phone having the same frequency as the trigger sensing it.

Ka-boom!

The explosion could be heard from the lobby and immediately sent a wave of panic to the people lingering there. A woman shrieked from impulse, quickly grabbing the arm of her husband like he was her Superman.

With the commotion going on outside and the sudden explosion inside, pandemonium was inevitable. The fire alarm sounded. Smoke started to billow from the stairway.

The doorman tried to take charge of the situation, directing everyone outside. "Everybody, please exit the building in an orderly fashion," he announced.

A few dozen folks hastily started to exit the building. Cristal was covertly mixed in with the exiting crowd, keeping her low profile intact.

Dozens of NYPD officers were everywhere, their marked cars engulfing the entire area, lights blaring from every direction, radios crackling. Shock and horror were registered on so many faces, the scene reminiscent of 9/11.

With the fire happening in the building across the street from where Chow Ling Tao's body lay, the peaceful event quickly transitioned into anarchy of epic proportions, turning Lincoln Center into Ground Zero.

Cristal easily slipped away from it all—job well done.

THIRTEEN

●●●●●●●●●●●●●●●●●●●●●●●●●●●●●●●●●●

I t was a long ride for Cristal, but it was also a relaxing one. The sun was rising gradually, spreading daylight across the sky. Cristal had gotten some needed sleep while riding on the Greyhound bus as the landscape changed from urban metropolis to rural area and back to the metropolis of Massachusetts. There weren't many passengers on the bus, so she had her own seat and time to think.

The Chow Ling Tao hit had gone smoothly, so it was time to get out of Dodge. Chow was an important figure, both politically and in the underworld, so there was no doubt that those devoted to him would come looking to avenge his murder, which happened right in front of his family.

She checked her bank account via cell phone. Her payment had already been transferred. Another body, another dollar.

She closed her eyes, feeling the bus driver navigate through narrow, winding roads. The engine snarled up steep hills, approaching their destination in great time,

New Bedford Ferry Terminal. The place looked almost historic with cobblestone buildings lining MacArthur Drive.

Located approximately seven miles off the southern coast of Cape Cod was Martha's Vineyard, where Cristal boarded the eighty-foot ferry carrying one hundred and thirty passengers to Vineyard Haven, a seaside village also known as Tisbury. With indoor and outdoor seating on the ferry, Cristal chose to sit outdoors beneath the blue sky and was treated to some of the best sightseeing on Buzzards Bay.

Stepping off the ferry with the other one hundred thirty passengers onto the island, Cristal headed toward one of the idling cabs waiting near the port. She was only one of a few young black faces sprinkled amongst a sea of Caucasian faces.

She climbed into a white cab with a white driver on Water Street and told him her destination. Fifteen minutes later, she arrived at a peaceful-looking beachfront cottage on Lagoon Pound Road.

She handed the driver a fifty-dollar bill for a twenty-dollar fare as she climbed out the backseat. "Keep the change," she told him.

"Thank you," he said, smiling.

After closing the cab door, she finally turned around and took in the beauty of it all—sun, water, sand, and sea. The cozy cottage was sizable and simplistic—a little old-fashioned white clapboard with shutters, a wraparound porch, a canopied swing off to one side, and a few steps up to the door. There was hardly any grass because it was mostly a meditation garden with little statuettes hidden near bushes. Purple, pink, yellow, and blue perennials added to the lush flora that draped, shaded, concealed, and beautified.

Cristal walked up the steps and entered the cottage like she owned the place. Inside, there was the smell of wild roses growing through the hawthorn hedge and the smell of timber. She could hear opera music playing from the rear of the cottage. The rooms were minimally furnished with just the bare necessities, but comfy.

She walked into a small back room overlooking a colorful garden. In the room a man sat quietly on a saddled seat counter stool, his right arm raised with a paintbrush between his thumb and his fingertip with him softly brushing against the white canvas attached to the easel in front of him. A wonderful picture of his garden was gradually coming to life with a kaleidoscope of color as Nicolai Gedda, the celebrated Swedish operatic tenor, delighted his ears from an antique record player.

"You don't knock first?" the man said without turning, his focus still on his artwork.

"Do I ever?"

"It's the polite thing to do."

"When have I ever been polite?"

"I could have had company," he said composedly.

"Then she would have to leave."

He grunted while touching up the amethyst flower in his painting, bringing out its star-shaped blooms of brilliant blue and sky blue, as well as violet and white. His talent with the paintbrush on the canvas was unquestionable.

"What brings you here?" he asked.

"I needed to get away." Cristal stood directly behind him, gazing at his artwork. She was impressed.

"To get away, huh? From the Chow hit?"

"You heard?"

"It's all over the news."

"I made sure to cover all my tracks."

"By coming here afterwards." He finally turned in his seat to face her.

"It's never been a problem with you before."

"It never is. Coming here once a month to escape is fine with me, but do not start making a habit of it," he said to her in a stern tone.

"I won't," she said.

He turned around to continue working with the brush.

"It's nice," she said, referring to his painting.

He didn't respond.

The Bishop, an aging, distinguished man with smooth, dark chocolate skin, a head full of stark white, wiry hair and a thick, grayish goatee, was Cristal's contact at GHOST Protocol. He had been born in Cuba to a Nigerian father and Cuban mother. He had come to the States in the late seventies when he was nine years old. He'd started out as muscle for a guerrilla pimp named Winter and was known and feared for his brutality against conflicting pimps and gang members.

During the mid-eighties, The Bishop was recruited by a drug cartel to become a triggerman because of his marksmanship and his knack for locating and terminating anyone where he found them, whether in public or private. He soon became a vicious hit man with a legendary reputation. Subsequently, his thirst for violence and his hardcore reputation landed him in a state prison, where he did a fifteen-year stint.

In the late nineties, he was scouted by GHOST Protocol to become an assassin for them. He'd worked his way up the ranks throughout the years and was highly respected. His name alone sanctioned fear in his victims and cohorts. His list of kills included warlords, politicians, drug dealers, kingpins, presidents of foreign countries, dictators, other assassins, and CEOs of billion-dollar companies.

The Bishop was able to keep a mental account of every kill he had made in two decades, and he was able to recount the details of each kill. How did he do it? He used a mnemonic device first used by Hippo, the ancient Greek philosopher. Using some article of personal import, he would mark it and mentally tell himself the story associated with that mark. Some assassins got a tattoo to commemorate each kill, but there was only so much skin available on the body. Anything tangible could be actionable evidence against them in court and be admitted to a grand jury: notes, journals, blog entries. One of his golden rules was to never write anything down. Ever! A notch in his memory was able to help him track his progress and remember his kill stories. Now, in his fifties, he no longer had to fulfill the contracts, only assign them.

The Bishop had been married three times and had three divorces and no children. He'd never learned how to display love. In his line of work, emotions were dangerous to have. Love could prove to be costly.

Most people who knew The Bishop thought he was the coldest thing around, from his eyes, his touch, and his mannerisms. He rarely smiled or joked. He was a wise man, spending most of his time away from it all. The painting and opera music relaxed him.

"Do you ever get out?"

He ignored her.

"How did you learn to paint so well?" she asked.

He continued to ignore her. He always behaved as if he was annoyed with her questions and meddling. He rarely had any visitors, and Martha's Vineyard, where the only access to the island was by ferry, was the perfect place for a retired killer.

Most people were fearful to be around him, afraid of his past, and terrified by his brooding personality, but Cristal wasn't afraid of, or intimidated, by him. Looking deeper into his eyes, she knew there was a layer of compassion within. She admired him. He appeared to have peace after all the murders he had committed. It was remarkable that he was able to adapt to a peaceful society, become a taxpaying citizen, and remain undetected by the locals.

Cristal turned and was about to exit the room when she suddenly heard him say, "I love to paint because it's a distraction from everything else in this crazy world."

"I see."

"You need to find your niche away from it all," he said.

"My niche? From what?"

"The place this life will take you if you don't know how to handle it."

Cristal listened willingly, knowing his history. He had been around and had survived it all—prison, numerous murder attempts against his life—and he had escaped prosecution and death by always being cautious.

"If you don't know how to escape from the murders, then it will consume you and tear you apart."

Though he'd always behaved like he was annoyed she was there, in honesty, he did enjoy her company. He saw something in her that he'd seen in himself years ago. She was special, and she was a survivor.

"When I found you, you were a wreck, Cristal. They wanted to forget about you, but I know determination, skills, and wit when I see it. And you had it. I vouched for you, and you came through. I knew you had the skills to be one of the best; that you wouldn't disappoint me."

Cristal was pleased to hear it. She remained nonchalant toward his comment, smiling inwardly. For The Bishop to say he was impressed with her was like a medal of honor. He rarely gave anyone praise.

"Thank you," she replied simply.

He touched up a few items on his painting and stood

up. He walked toward her and looked at her. Though her face was scarred a little, and her eyes were filled with coldness and pain, she still had beauty in her. She had eyes like a warrior. For him, it was rare to see eyes like hers in a young woman.

"I need to make a run to the store," he said. "You feel like taking a ride with me?"

"Why not?"

They exited the cottage and walked toward his white Jeep Wrangler. Clad in his cargo shorts, white shirt, and sandals, The Bishop looked like a normal, everyday American enjoying the life of retirement.

"Hey, Mrs. Dearman," he said to an elderly white woman tending to her garden in front of her home.

She quickly smiled and waved back. "How are you, Sam?" she hollered.

"How are those violets coming along?"

"They're coming along great. I'm keeping them in moist soil and trying not to let them dry out, like you suggested."

"That's good, that's good," The Bishop replied dynamically.

Mrs. Dearman's eyes landed on Cristal.

The Bishop quickly said, "My granddaughter."

"Oh hello," she greeted.

Cristal faintly waved. She was taken aback by The Bishop's sudden change. He seemed like a completely different person. *What gives?* She wondered. Why was he so out in the open and chatty with his neighbors? A man like him, a stone-cold killer, wouldn't he be a bit more secluded and standoffish? Wasn't he afraid of his past catching up to him?

She climbed into the passenger seat of his Wrangler. In all her visits, this was the first time they were leaving the cottage to go elsewhere. He moved like he had always been a civilian here, all of his life.

The Wrangler rounded the narrow curve on Weaver Lane, thick trees and shrubberies on both sides of the road. They rode in silence for a moment. She took in the scenery. It was a different world from everything she was used to.

They pulled up to a fruit stand fifteen miles from his home. The open-air business venue that sold seasonal fruit was nestled in suburbia, on a side road, and was teeming with people going through and selecting quality fresh fruit and vegetables.

Cristal and The Bishop climbed out of the Wrangler and joined the others in the market. As they walked around, he was greeted warmly by the other locals, even the owner of the stand. The atmosphere, reminded her of the sitcom *Cheers*, "where everybody knows your name," and The Bishop was Norm.

The owner, a short, round man with a natural smile and thinning gray hair, said, "We got some fresh mangoes in last night, Sam. I saved a few on the side for you, knowing how fast they can go, and how you love first pick."

"You're the best, Mike."

The Bishop grabbed a plastic bag, and, with Cristal following behind him, started slowly going through the aisles, which were filled with an assortment of colorful fruits, vegetables, and snacks. He inspected each piece of fruit thoroughly before dropping them into his bag.

"I know what you're thinking," he said out the blue.

"What's that?"

"How did I go to The Bishop, from Sam?"

"It came across my mind."

He picked up an apple, looked at it for a moment, and continued talking to her without looking her way. "It can be a hard transition if you make it that way."

"Well, explain it to me."

"Not here."

Cristal didn't push for an answer, knowing The Bishop always did things on his time.

They continued shopping for fresh fruit. He had a thing for mangoes and pears. He was healthy and fit for his age. His physique was still impressive. If he wanted to, he was able to take out a dozen men with his bare hands.

The Bishop once preached to his apprentices, including Cristal, "Equality is for the weak and stupid. It's about pulling the trigger, simple as that. One finger, one movement."

The Bishop paid for his fruit with cash and went back to his truck. He started the ignition and drove off.

Cristal thought, *Is this a cover, or is this really him, someone new and transformed? Does he worry about his old life catching up to him?*

Riding the same road back to his cottage, he said to her, "Natalia was supposed to come see me today."

"So where is she?"

"Her plans changed. She'll come next Tuesday, like planned."

Natalia was his girlfriend from Boston. A few years older than Cristal, she was beautiful and intelligent, with a shy smile and a warm heart. She was a business graduate from Harvard. Cristal didn't know anything about her and had never seen her, but The Bishop spoke about her every now and again. She would come over twice a week always on Tuesdays and Saturdays and spend the night with him. She would cook for him, wash his clothes, and make strong, passionate love to him.

Cristal was happy to learn he had someone special in his life. Even an ex-killer like The Bishop had needs too.

They talked more on their way back to his cottage about the business of killing. It was only them, in a moving Jeep out in the open, in a calm vicinity, and having trust between the new school and the old school.

He said to her, "If you want to make killing your business, you have to treat it like a business."

It wasn't the first time she'd heard those same words from The Bishop. He knew that for a scarred woman like Cristal, in most cases, it wasn't hard to take a life when a life had been taken from someone. It wasn't about embracing revenge, but nurturing hatred.

"Some of you young assassins, y'all get sloppy and gaudy, running and zooming around in speedboats and fast cars, or rappelling down the faces of tall buildings. Myself, I've quietly interrupted my target's Starbucks run with a quick double-tap to the back of their head. They never saw me coming. I'm in, I'm out, shots off, target down, move subtly, and then I'm on to my next job. That's the work ethic that got me to where I am today."

He smoothly wheeled the Wrangler around the steep curve like a professional racecar driver, one hand on the steering wheel, the other on the gear shift, shifting with no uncertainty about veering off the road.

"You know how I survived? How I'm able to fit in?" He glanced at Cristal, maybe looking for a response from her. "I've maintained a balance of work and life."

Cristal nodded.

"I've been killing people for more than thirty-three years. There's no denying that rising to the top takes commitment and sacrifice. Killing people has to be the first priority, but does it have to be the only priority?"

Cristal didn't know the answer, so she chose to listen, rather than intervene with her own two cents.

"Consider this," he said. "A woman, Elizabeth, works all her life, beginning with a summer paper route when she is twelve years old. By the time she's sixteen, she's working two jobs, babysitting on the weekends and working after school as a supermarket cashier. She graduates college summa cum laude with a double major and never looks back. At forty she's acquired wealth, respect, two dogs, and a career. She has all the trappings of success but no one to share it with. Is she happy?

"Let's consider this second scenario. Jenny married straight out of high school to the quarterback. By the time she's twenty-one, she has two kids, at twenty-five she has four. In their late twenties, her husband begins to feel like he'd made a mistake marrying so young and takes out his frustration on his wife with a couple backhand slaps across her face. He's a womanizer, although he tries to hide his discretions. At thirty, he no longer cares to cover up his affairs, and the children become privy to his adulterous ways. On Jenny's fortieth birthday she smiles as she's surrounded by her husband, kids, family and friends. To the people on the outside looking in, she has what most women want. She is a housewife with four loving children and a husband. Jenny has a family, but is she happy?"

The Bishop took the next corner at 35mph. He had control over the winding roads, knowing the area like the back of his hand.

Cristal held onto the overhead bar of the Jeep for support, with the doors being off and the steady, jerking movement making her rock from side to side. She didn't answer the question, knowing it was rhetorical.

"This is what I'm trying to tell you. Those were just two examples of an unbalanced life. The key to happiness is creating the life you want to live."

He pulled up to his cozy, comfortable cottage nestled away from the city. Before exiting the Jeep, he looked at Cristal seriously. "You can't pull the trigger if you got the shakes, so never stress yourself."

The Bishop was always full of advice, trying to school Cristal, reminding her to never get sloppy. He even informed her how grimy and treacherous the Commission was. They lure in unsuspecting recruits, tantalize them with large figures in an overseas bank account, and when they turn twenty-five and expect to age out, they're murdered without a dime to their name. She was floored by the news when she first heard it.

FOURTEEN

●●●●●●●●●●●●●●●●●●●●●●●●●●●●●●●●●●●●●●

Tamar had carefully checked Melissa's SoHo apartment, but to no avail. It seemed like she had vacated the apartment a few days earlier. Now, she skillfully picked the lock to the front door of her next option, the Boston apartment, and she cautiously entered the spacious oasis.

Tamar slowly crept into the lavish Brookline condo, located a stone's throw from Fenway Park. The beautifully decorated 1,375-square-foot, two-bedroom condo had artwork hung in the long hallway and the latest amenities. Melissa Chin was living well from her book sales. Dressed in all black, a silencer-equipped .45 in one hand and a goody bag of torture devices in the other, she went through the apartment room by room. She was in the mood to extract information from the author the hard way, yearning to know how she was able to write about herself and the Cristal Clique. Where did she get the information? Who was she?

The master bedroom was Tamar's last stop. She went searching through the large closet, looked underneath the king-size bed, and tossed aside the tufted gold chairs. Nothing.

The entire apartment was clean—no signs of life— except for another note written by Melissa Chin. It read:

A DAY LATE, A DOLLAR SHORT, SORRY FOR YOUR MISS. BETTER LUCK NEXT TIME!

Scowling, Tamar smashed the large flat-screen TV to the floor. Boiling over from rage, she crumpled the piece of paper into her fist. Someone knew she was coming, and she wondered who. Someone else was pulling the strings and making her look really bad to E.P. and the Commission. Every day Melissa Chin remained alive was a day of agony for Tamar.

Leaving the apartment, Tamar had an afterthought before climbing into her car. She lifted her head and gazed up at the condo. It didn't make sense.

Could they be setting me up? Why?

Maybe E.P. was messing with her head, fucking with her mind, making her chase a ghost. *What if Melissa Chin is actually E.P.? Being intimate with Cristal, he could have known all the details about her life and mine.*

It made sense.

She had to think. She had to be smart. There wasn't any room for error. She removed a cigarette from her dwindling pack and lit it up, taking a much needed-pull of nicotine, allowing the tobacco to cool her nerves. She exhaled the smoke and lingered near her black Volvo, her conventional ride around Boston.

She couldn't dwell on Melissa Chin for long, since the

Commission had assigned her to a new target, a Mexican drug lord named Hector Guzman.

The last thing Tamar wanted was another drug lord to assassinate. She had killed so many of them, it was easy as swatting flies on the front porch in the south. Too easy. There was nothing praiseworthy about killing these stupid, gaudy men who thought hiding behind their goons and armor-plated vehicles made them untouchable.

What Tamar craved was someone who mattered internationally; maybe taking out a president of a country, even the president of the United States. She wanted to leave her calling card globally, travel all over the world. Anywhere but America. Just as in the book *Killer Dolls*. E.P. had promised these things would come, but yet nothing. He wasn't keeping his word. But she continued to be loyal to him and the organization.

•••

The Green Dragon was a fairly small place. During the day, sunshine poured in through the large windows, but it got noisy fast. Patriots and Celtics fans found it a popular Boston bar to hang out, drink, and root for the home team. The small Boston bar by the waterfront was filling up fast as it neared midnight, almost reaching full capacity. The balmy weather made sitting outside by the waters pleasant.

The place was lively with the live band on the stage. The band was loud, soulful, and energetic as they performed one of their own songs, making the people dance and drink more. The lead singer was shirtless, heavily tattooed, and was moving around the stage animatedly, his vocals screaming into the microphone as he played his guitar.

Hordes of college kids were there getting pissy drunk, and a few cute girls in their bohemian outfits and partying attitude were becoming extra friendly and flirtatious with the young and old males in the area.

Tamar sat at the corner of the bar, downing a few vodka shots, removed from all the activity around her. She had a lot on her mind. She hated Boston with their ugly accents, confusing street layouts, bigotry, and terrible driving. But she wasn't in any rush to leave right away.

"Can I buy you another drink, beautiful?" a man asked from behind her. "Looks like you could use some company."

No matter how discreet Tamar tried to be, she was still a very pretty girl. She felt his hand against her waist, and he was already trying to massage her side without asking her first.

She turned around on her barstool to take in his appearance. Gazing at her was a six foot two mammoth of a man—tall, black, and not so handsome. He had intense eyes, and his voice was deep and brooding. He could easily intimidate anyone in the room with his thuggish, hardcore appearance.

Tamar deduced a few things about him. He had done some time in prison. He wore a sleeveless shirt, and his jailhouse tattoos were obvious and poorly done, and he probably didn't do too well with the ladies, because he looked like he didn't take no for an answer.

She looked him up and down from head to toe. He was clad in stripes and plaid together and white socks with flip-flops.

Ewwww!

Despite his tacky appearance and rough pickup line, Tamar decided to give him the time of day. Bored, she wanted to make the best out of her trip to Boston.

"You wanna be my company tonight?" she asked.

"Hells, yeah," he said. "A beautiful woman like you and a fine man like me? Shit, the magic we could make? Wicked!"

He was corny, but he was keeping her somewhat entertained.

"I'll take another shot of vodka," she said.

"Vodka, huh? Okay."

He signaled for the bartender, and she ordered her drink.

Tamar noticed a few ladies gawking her way, not with jealousy, but more like a warning, like they knew something about this guy she didn't.

"By the way, I'm Jake."

"Sandy," she lied.

They shook hands, and it looked like a bond was made.

Tamar tossed the shot down her throat and smiled his way. She was flirtatious and touchy-feely with him, which gave him the confidence to place his hand against her thigh and massage between her legs. She let it slide, knowing he was a pervert.

"Excuse me, I have to use the ladies' room," she said. She removed herself from his presence and went into the bathroom.

She wasn't even in the bathroom a minute before a young lady approached her while she checked her image in the mirror.

"Be careful around him," the girl warned. "He's bad news. He's a monster."

Tamar looked at the petite, young woman and already knew she'd had a bad incident with Jake. Rape and abuse, maybe. Whatever it was, she took it upon herself to warn Tamar. But Tamar already knew what she was getting into.

Tamar smirked at the girl. "Sweetheart, I don't need any warnings. I can handle myself, and I can handle him." She pivoted away from the girl and walked away. She wasn't a weak bitch and was ready to show it.

She met up with Jake again. "You wanna get out of here?"

He quickly nodded, uttering out, "Hells, yeah!" He dropped a twenty-dollar bill on the bar countertop and couldn't wait to get to his place fast enough.

He slid into a beat-up pickup truck, and she climbed into her Volvo. She followed him to his home in West End, Boston, a vibrant, ethnically diverse neighborhood tucked behind Beacon Hill. On Storrow Drive, a sign outside the West End Condominiums and Apartments read: If you lived here, you'd be home now.

Tamar paid close attention to her surroundings, like she was trained to do. She was by the river, and it seemed like a quiet neighborhood. She continued driving behind the pickup, which finally came to a stop in front of a building that looked like it had been nice in the past, but needed some urgent repairs. She parked close to the pickup and stepped out, swiveling her head from left to right, looking and watching.

Jake climbed out of his truck. "Home sweet home."

It was far from home, but it would do.

Before she could step inside the building, Jake was already becoming an octopus, touching and grabbing private places. Tamar played along, transitioning into a meek, flirtatious character, giggling and laughing. Up close, he was a big and solid dude, so she knew, once inside his apartment, anything goes.

Inside his place was a train wreck. The place was messy and sparsely furnished with tattered couches, a rickety table, frayed carpeting, and exposed wiring. The walls were peeling off, and an odor of stale cigarette smoke lingered. The master bedroom had a soiled mattress in the corner near the window and dilapidated dressers with missing drawers, and the bathroom didn't have a toilet seat.

He shut the door and locked it. He smiled waywardly her way, grabbing his crotch. "You ready to have some fun? You're the prettiest girl I ever brought here." He was already unzipping his jeans.

Tamar stood in the center of the living room, looking assertive and ready. She was far from flattered by his statement, but she expected this type of behavior from him.

"And what if I say no . . . let's just talk, get to know each other."

"Talk? I know you didn't come here to talk. And the best way for me to get to know you is being inside you."

"Oh, really?"

He pulled out his flaccid dick. He was hung like a horse, but that didn't impress Tamar. He stepped closer, stroking his flaccid penis into a long, hard erection, licking his lips.

Tamar took a few steps back from his threatening approach. He'd done this before, rape or forced entry. She knew any unfortunate girl he brought back to his apartment didn't leave until she had a hard dick thrust inside of her.

He unhooked his belt and came closer. "I knew the minute I saw you, I wanted you. I know that pussy is tight and nice for Jake," he said, referring to himself in the third person. "Let me see that body."

"And once again, what if I said no?" Tamar said evenly, toying with him.

His lecherous smile could send fear through any woman, but Tamar remained cool and reserved. He went for her, reaching out for her arm suddenly, his hard dick still gripped in his fist as he jerked himself off.

Tamar stepped back quickly, just out of his grasp.

"You think you have a choice? I know you're teasing me, bitch," he growled. "You wanna fuck; you wouldn't have come here if you didn't. You know what it is."

"Let's play a game."

"A game?"

"Yes, a game," she repeated, smirking his way.

"The only game I'm interested in is the one between your legs."

"Well, unless you play this game with me, then you can't have me."

He chuckled with a steely glare at her. "Bitch, I don't have time to play games. I wanna fuck you."

"You can't have me."

"Oh, you think?"

He lunged toward her, but Tamar swiftly sidestepped his charge, tripped him up, and sent him stumbling forward into the couch.

He was clearly embarrassed.

"You ready to play my game?" she repeated calmly.

"Fuck your game!"

"Then you can't fuck me."

Jake stood up and charged at her again. Tamar foiled his attack again, spinning around and kicking him in the back, sending him flying into the floor.

"You're a big boy," she said. "A girl needs to be careful around you."

Jake screamed from pure frustration.

"Now, are you ready to play my game?" she asked simply, grinning down at him.

He stood up and towered over her. Scowling, he clenched his fists, his eyes brimming with anger.

"Now, the rules to my game. You take me out, then it's all yours—pussy, my mouth, even my ass—no limits."

He laughed. "You serious?"

"Like a heart attack."

"You want to wrestle with me?"

"Like WWF, sweetheart," she replied.

Jake smiled. He was sure he could easily take her down. He figured one punch from him would have her unconscious. Unconscious or not, he was going to fuck her.

Tamar was ready to show off her skills and have some fun with him. It had been a while since she'd had any hand-to-hand combat. She needed the exercise. Besides, tonight, Jake needed to be taught a lesson. His brutal way with women was about to come to an end.

Before Jake could move, she moved swiftly and punched him with her closed left fist full across his face, rocking him.

He took a step back and then steadied himself, blinking his eyes and staring at her. He didn't even see that simple move coming. Blood trickled from his lips. He licked it away quickly and said, "Oh, I'm gonna definitely have some fun with you."

He threw a punch, and she dodged it, and then she retaliated with a swift kick into his side, her shin crashing against his ribs.

Jake tumbled backwards from the whack, and she punched him again, this time with her right fist to his jaw, causing him to stagger forward. He remained on his feet, blinking heavily.

"You still wanna play?"

"You're mine, bitch!" he hollered.

He stood erect again, his face flaring up like a firecracker, while Tamar stood ten feet from him, still looking unperturbed.

Jake charged like a bull, ready to impale his fists through Tamar, but she rolled her hands down and away with a minor Wing Chun deflection, and snapped his head back hard, popping his jaw like a rat trap.

He flicked again, and this time, Tamar hit him in the Adam's apple. He clutched his throat, his face turning bright red.

"You still wanna play?"

It took him a moment to regain his composure and rise to his feet. Like a brute, he shook off the pain. He charged again like a fool.

This time she lifted herself vertically, with him rushing forward, and smashed an elbow into the side of his skull, the soft spot high on the temple. It sent him crashing face-first into the floor, this time leaving him completely dazed.

Tamar went over to him while he rolled over onto his back and slapped her right palm down on his face, shattering his nose. Blood spewed everywhere.

He hollered.

She looked delighted. "Are you having fun yet?"

He hunched over, on his knees, his blood leaking onto the frayed carpet. He was clearly no match for Tamar. But he wasn't about to give up, not yet.

"You're dead, bitch!" he hollered, his mouth and nose coated with blood. He suddenly had a knife. "I'm gonna cut you up really good, you bitch."

Tamar moved away from him. She now had to be extra careful. But she wasn't afraid.

As he started toward her, she took another step back and slid her belt out of her pant loops. She looped it around her left hand so that the buckle end swung loose.

Jake pounced toward her wildly, swinging and throwing the knife madly her way, and she moved away from the sharp blade with precision.

Finally, she went from playing defense to offense, hitting him with the belt buckle in the back of his head. Then when he tripped up, she hit him with a left hand in the *V* under his ribs, where the sternum ends, paralyzing his diaphragm.

He doubled over, gasping, and then pitched forward onto the floor. He couldn't move. His blood continued to drip as he exhaled and inhaled. He inched his arms under himself and pushed himself up on his hands and knees with his head hanging like a winded horse.

Smirking at the defeated brute, Tamar stood over her handiwork. "Guess you don't want this pussy bad enough, huh?"

Jake couldn't speak. He was done for.

"You thought I was like them—fuckin' weak. You thought you were about to take this pussy like you did the others, huh?"

He didn't answer. He could barely move.

"How many women have you taken advantage of? Raped and abused? Took something from them because you thought you could, using your size and strength to dominate them?"

He didn't answer.

"This was fun, though. I haven't had this much fun in a while."

"Please," he finally managed to utter.

"Please? You want mercy from me?"

As Jake stared up at her, suddenly looking defeated and pitiful, Tamar raised her heeled shoe and slammed it into his jaw. The only sound beyond the crack of his skull on the ground was the soft exhalation that escaped his lips.

He whimpered like a bitch.

Tamar wasn't done with him yet. She didn't come to Boston to leave empty-handed. Since she couldn't get Melissa Chin, he would do. She had a bag of goodies in her car, and they were about to be put to good use tonight. She was about to make tonight the worst night of his life, a night he would never forget. And she planned on leaving with a parting gift afterwards—his testicles.

FIFTEEN

●●●●●●●●●●●●●●●●●●●●●●●●●●●●●●●●●●●●

It was another long bus ride for Cristal into North Carolina on the Greyhound. It would be another three hours before the bus reached the city of Charlotte. Cristal had some things on her mind, and she simply wanted to get away for a while. She sat in the rear of the bus, in a window seat. Next to her sat an elderly Hispanic male in his late seventies. Like her, he mostly slept during the trip, and chatter between them was thin.

The sun was gradually breaking open the sky, the dawn's light burning the darkness away. She gazed out the bus window and watched as the large glowing sphere rose slowly into the dull morning sky. The sun dispersed its beams in every direction, illuminating the small town they were passing through.

She thought about The Bishop and his words. She left his place feeling like a better and more resourceful woman. She'd spent two days with him then left with some peace of mind, if she could call it that. The Bishop had survived this long and was living a content life, so she wanted to follow his every footstep.

She took in everything he'd said to her. His words were rooted into her mind. *Find your niche in life, outside of killing. Assassins could never retire; they just become more-difficult-to-kill targets. Maintain a balance of work and life.*

Cristal felt she had found that balance in her life in Charlotte, North Carolina. His name was Daniel Roberts. They'd been dating for six months now. He was a medical student at Johnson C. Smith University, in his fourth year and on a partial scholarship. So with a few student loans that needed to be paid off, he had to work two jobs and attend school full-time.

Daniel was from New Orleans, and had survived Katrina and poverty before that. He was a nerd, and Cristal fell in love with him, though not right away.

•••

They met while she was doing a hit in Raleigh, North Carolina, the Benson Okeke contract. Benson was a foreign diplomat from Western Africa—a warlord and brutal savage who'd murdered millions of his own people in civil warfare.

She'd executed that contract, assassinating him in a crowded restaurant while he was seated in the VIP area with his armed goons. She narrowly escaped them, ditching her disguise and immediately changing her look as they were dead on her heels.

She ran into the busy street and into a nearby bar. Knowing the bodyguards were looking for a single black woman, she purposely took a seat next to Daniel on the barstool as he was watching a sports event on the mounted TV. She quickly started a conversation with him, making it look like they'd known each other for a while and were two people having a drink, enjoying each other's company.

He was caught off guard, but went with the flow.

It worked, and she eluded the bodyguards.

She lingered at the bar for a moment, conversing with Daniel, and surprisingly, they were having an intellectual conversation. Though they came from different worlds, they found themselves talking about sports, food, and movies.

Then it was Cristal who was surprisingly caught off guard. He actually was making her laugh and smile.

Daniel was in Raleigh for a book signing. Harriet A. Washington, the author of the book *Medical Apartheid*, was in town. As a medical student and a devotee of black history and medicine, he thought the book about the Tuskegee syphilis experiment was a must-read. He couldn't miss the opportunity to meet the Black American writer, winner of the 2007 National Book Critics Circle Award for nonfiction.

Cristal was intrigued by his knowledge, his humor, and warm attitude toward a stranger he had just met. And he didn't seem to mind the minor scars on her face. Daniel gazed at her like she was the queen of Egypt, and he wasn't shy in telling her so.

Cristal remained vague about her life, while knowing everything about him. She wouldn't give him her heart so easily. Despite his easygoing and jovial way of thinking, it was still hard for her to trust anyone. When he tried to make plans for the future, she was always hesitant to commit, knowing his world and hers could clash. So he learned to live spontaneously with her.

Cristal was unable to love after Tamar took everything from her. Her best friend had betrayed her, leading to months of isolation and fear. She didn't believe in tomorrow, but The Bishop and especially Daniel allowed her to open her heart again, making her think that maybe she could have a tomorrow.

•••

The sky had been a postcard-perfect day. The bus was an hour from Charlotte, and like her mood, the weather above began to change. She peered out the window. The sky was now tar-black, and the large clouds were moving over the vast region. She sighed. She didn't have an umbrella on her.

Half an hour away from the city, Cristal heard tapping on the window, and then it became a pitter-patter. It started to downpour. She stared at the bad weather as the Greyhound bus made its way closer to the bus station. She could hear the murmuring of the rain through the window. On the highway, the roofs of the cars danced with spray from the rainstorm.

As the bus rolled toward the bus station on Tryon Street, she could see Daniel waiting for her by his car, an aged Honda Civic. He was a sweetheart, standing by his car in the rain under an umbrella.

Seeing him, her smile came naturally. He wore glasses and had a small, curly Afro. He was slim with a peanut-butter complexion, no facial hair at all, and handsome. She couldn't help but to think of him as the black Bill Gates. He was very intelligent and wanted to become a brain surgeon.

As the bus pulled into the station, the rain began to let up. The sun came out again, casting slanted beams of light across the city.

Cristal never took her eyes off her man. With just one small duffel bag, she got off the bus and hurried toward him, smiling. He started her way, and she went into his open arms where he hugged her lovingly and didn't hesitate to say, "I missed you."

"I missed you too," she said.

They hugged each other strongly, and then they kissed. She had been away from him for two months.

Looking into her face, he asked, "So, how was Africa, Beatrice?"

"It was an experience," she replied. "I can't wait to tell you all about it."

"I can't wait to hear about it," he said, looking at her with enthusiasm. He hugged her again, reluctant to let her go.

Cristal was trained to conjure up false identities to make her fraudulent life believable to anyone. She had told him her name was Beatrice Thompson, Bee for short. He also thought she worked for the Peace Corps, which allowed her to travel to different countries around the world to aid others in need. It was a life-defining experience. She wanted to contribute to improving the lives of others. It was the perfect cover story. It allowed her to be gone for long periods of time and off grid without him able to keep in contact with her all the time.

When Daniel had asked about her minor scars when they'd first met, she said, "I got them while I was in Uganda, in a small town called Gulu. I was helping with the medical supplies for the children in an IDP camp, where there was an ebola outbreak.

"I was getting to know the Acholi people very well. We became a family. But the hostility between the UPDF and the LRA was growing. One night, there was an explosion, then heavy gunfire. I tried to hurry the children onto the buses for escape and was wounded from the gunfire."

Daniel believed every word of it. He'd never met a woman her age so knowledgeable on so many topics. For him, it was love at first sight.

She did feel a slight twinge of guilt around Daniel. He was a nice guy, truthful and always loving, no matter if it was a sunny day or a cloudy day. Daniel had the type of attitude that could strengthen a feather to lift a ton of stone up a hill like the stone was light as feather itself.

"Let me take this," he offered, taking the duffel bag from her hands.

She walked behind him, taking a deep breath then exhaling. She planned on being Beatrice for the next week or two. It felt good to become somebody different. She didn't want to think about New York or the Syndicate. She just wanted to escape.

She climbed into the passenger seat of his Civic, and Daniel started the ignition and drove off. While driving, he took her left hand into his and glanced at her with a warm smile. "I have missed you so much," he said. "I couldn't stop thinking about you since you've been gone. I'm glad you came back to me safe and sound."

Cristal smiled. His voice was sweet and velvety, like chocolate. She could listen to him talk all day, especially about his field in medicine and the brain and how it works.

•••

Daniel had wanted to become a neurologist since he was twelve years old. When he was eleven, his father died from brain cancer. He was close to his father, who'd had a large primary brain tumor. Daniel felt helpless that he couldn't prevent his father's death. It changed him. He wanted to save lives, so he studied everything he knew about the brain. He wanted to be trained in the diagnosis and treatment of nervous system disorders, including diseases of the brain, spinal cord, nerves, and muscles.

Through him, Cristal was also learning about the mind and medicine. He was educating her.

He asked her one time, "Did you know that fruit flies have been extensively studied to gain insight into the role of genes in brain development?"

Cristal shook her head.

"Also, the brain is an organ that serves as the center of the nervous system in all vertebrate and most invertebrate animals, and guess what?"

"What?" Cristal smiled, loving his mind and passion for the brain, and how he could go on and on to talk about it in a way that even made her interested in it.

"There are only a few invertebrates such as sponges, jellyfish, adult sea squirts, and starfish that do not have a brain, even if diffuse neural tissue is present," he explained.

She did not know that either.

Their first week dating, he talked about how the brain was the most complex organ in a vertebrate's body.

"You see, in a typical human, the cerebral cortex, which is the largest part, is estimated to contain fifteen to thirty-three billion neurons, and each connected by synapses to several thousand other neurons."

An intelligent and motivated man is so sexy.

Coming from New Orleans, Daniel grew up in poverty and in the ghetto. His father was a janitor and a voracious reader, and his mother was a housewife, and they both provided Daniel with love and care.

After his father's death, he and his mother moved in with his mother's sister. During Katrina, he worked with FEMA to help bring his community back to life and help others those trapped or wounded. His warm heart and generosity were inherited from his parents. He brought back a piece of Cristal that she thought had been lost forever.

•••

Daniel pulled up to his one-bedroom apartment in Belmont, a small suburban city in Gaston County, North Carolina, fifteen miles west of uptown Charlotte and nine miles east of Gastonia. Looking like Mayberry with its small population, it was the perfect place for Cristal to hide and experience the love and romance from her man.

Daniel carried her bag to his place on the first floor. It wasn't anything fancy, but mostly modest and affordable on his salary. Some would call his place a shotgun house: a narrow rectangular domestic residence, twelve feet wide, with rooms arranged one behind the other and doors at each end of the apartment.

Cristal went from staying at the Waldorf in New York City, to a cozy cottage in Martha's Vineyard, to an apartment looking like it came straight from "*Good Times* meets a backwoods family in the South."

"Welcome to my castle," Daniel joked.

Cristal laughed. "It's always perfect."

"Especially when you're in it with me," he said.

She smiled at his flattering comment. He was always praising her in different ways. His soothing words took her out of the harsh reality of killing and into a blissful certainty while with him.

Though she had the means for them to live really well, she rather enjoyed the life she'd created with him. They enjoyed cheap takeout from different places, or at times they'd have a home-cooked meal. His furniture was secondhand, the rickety floorboards were a little dusty, the apartment needed a paint job, and it was common to see a mouse or a roach now and again, but it was his home. A place where she felt wanted and safe.

The minute she stepped into his apartment, she plopped down on the old brown couch near the kitchen and propped her feet on the end of it. She closed her eyes and wanted to dream.

Daniel soon joined her on the couch, removed her shoes, and started to massage her feet. His fingers strummed her toes, making her smile and chuckle.

He then worked his way up her shins, the back of her thighs, and was now giving her a much-needed shoulder massage as she sat on the floor between his legs with her back against the couch.

Cristal cooed from his gentle touch. It was a great way to help her relax. "Oh, I so needed this."

"I know you did, baby, I know you did."

Through her shirt, she could feel his concentrated touch. He did her neck and upper back.

She removed her shirt, clad in her bra, and with that Daniel applied a small amount of oil. He started using sweeping strokes of his palms over her upper back and shoulders. He worked from her center and up. He plucked the tops of her shoulders from near the neck to her deltoids, holding the top of her shoulder between his thumb and index finger, supporting with the other three fingers, and then he gently pulled up and away.

"Daniel, you're the best."

He smiled. It was fun pleasing his woman.

He continued massaging her into an idyllic state, resting his fingers on the tops of her shoulder, making circular movements with his thumbs on either side of the spine, again working up and out. Subsequently, he supported her forehead with one palm and put his index finger and thumb around the back of her neck, pulling toward the back of her neck fairly gently, doing it up and down her neck.

Cristal found herself drifting away from his tender touch. One pleasant move was followed up by another, this time with Daniel's hands in the same position, trying to find her occipital ridge on the back of her skull, using the same index finger and thumb, one on each side of the center. He worked around her ridges doing tiny circles. He knew the complete anatomy of her body, where to put pressure and how to massage it. His hands against her felt like platinum.

For almost an hour, he continued to satisfy Cristal with his hands, doing a bit more plucking on the shoulders, a few more circles with his thumbs on her back, and then he finished his massage with some effleurage, leading up to the tops of her shoulders, then firmly down her arms and off the elbows.

By the time he was done, Cristal was fast asleep on the floor.

SIXTEEN

●●●●●●●●●●●●●●●●●●●●●●●●●●●●●●●●

The sunset was drinking what was left of a hot day, quenching its thirst before nightfall. Cristal and Daniel were relaxing over the hillside, where they decided to picnic together on a grassy field and watch the sun fall behind the horizon, the aura a prism spectrum with blended edges of streaking color. It looked like someone had poured a mixture of orange and red over the sky. As the sun descended, the sky became almost a muted brown.

Together, they ate turkey and cheese sandwiches and drank cheap champagne from the local store. It wasn't much, but she truly enjoyed it.

Nestled in his arms, and enjoying the moment of tranquility and picturesque setting, she sighed all of a sudden.

"What's wrong, baby?" he asked.

"Nothing."

"You sure?"

"Yes, I'm sure."

"You know you can talk to me about anything," he said. "No matter what it is, I'm here."

The corners of her mouth turned upwards faintly. She wished it were true. The one good person in her life, and she was lying to him about everything. Sometimes it was hard to look squarely at Daniel.

What if he knew the truth about her, how would he react? Could he handle knowing that the woman he wanted to marry one day was a coldblooded assassin with anxiety issues and other things? She was a real-life version of Charlene Elizabeth "Charly" Baltimore from the movie *The Long Kiss Goodnight*.

Cristal adjusted herself while still situated comfortably in his arms so she could softly look him in his eyes. "Daniel, don't ever change. You're a really good guy."

"You think?" he joked.

"You know you're a good guy. You're terrific."

"And you're a beautiful and great woman yourself, Bee. That's why I love you, because you're different. You're kind and kindhearted. How you're able to volunteer overseas in these diseased, war-torn countries, risk your life to help others. Not too many women can do what you do. Don't ever change who you are. Together, I feel we both can change the world."

"Change the world, huh? You and me."

"Yup, we're both good people that can make a difference to anything if we put our minds to it. And once I become a brain surgeon and make lots of money, I can contribute to the needy with both my hands and my pockets. I want to pour my riches into charities, and one day start my own."

"Good people, huh?" she said softly.

"Good people, yes, like in the Bible, the meek shall inherit the earth. We're the ones that are going to change the world, Bee," he said with conviction.

Cristal wanted to believe it with him. But she had seen the world for what it truly was, corrupted and damned. It felt like there was more evil in the world than good, and she had become a part of that evil, and actually experienced that evil when she witnessed her entire family being killed.

"But what if the good is not strong enough to handle the evil?" she said. "I've seen the real world, Daniel. I've seen how mankind works, and most time it's not a pretty picture. The evil out there, it has no limits."

"You got to have faith, baby. Faith, that's the root to change. This world, especially America, it needs to change. If not, then we will all drown in its iniquity. Do you know that America is a nation deeply rooted in violence? This country holds the distinction of being the wealthiest nation on the planet, but it is also one of the most violent. Baby, you know I'm against violence and bloodshed, I hate it. I've seen the aftermath of Katrina, how we treat our own, the destruction and deaths, and I was appalled by it all. It's one of the reasons why I wanted to become a doctor. I want to change people's lives for the better, give people hope when times can be desperate."

"It's the sins of our Founding Fathers," Cristal said. "This country was founded on violence and bloodshed. It's soaked in the blood of its original inhabitants, those who fought to steal their land, and those enslaved to build it."

"And that's why I'm pushing for a change. I want to make our people aware of our history, where we've been and where we need to go. I don't know how it's going to be done yet, but it will be done."

Daniel's drive and determination to make the world a better place someday was fascinating. He was someone special, not just in her life, but for the future. Men like Daniel rarely came along. She believed he had a calling.

They continued talking until dusk came, and then they packed up their little picnic area and walked back to the car. They laughed and played around with each other. She chased him around the open field, and then he chased her. They looked like two innocent children on a grassy playground in the night, in their own world, making each other happy, their eyes lit up with thrill and joy.

Cristal couldn't remember a time when she'd laughed so hard and felt so free.

Daniel grabbed her into his arms, twirling her around near his car. "I love you."

"I love you too," she said.

They kissed passionately under a full-moon night. A look between them, with a moment of silence, sparked something, creating an explosion of desire as both of their eyes spoke volumes. They no longer had to say a word to each other, reading what the other was thinking. They didn't want this day or this night to ever end.

Daniel made her feel like a woman again, a feeling she had been missing for a very long time. Even when she was with E.P., she never felt anything like this.

He smiled. She smiled.

"You ready?" he asked.

"Yes, I am."

A short time later, back at his place, they snuggled beneath a warm blanket as the atmosphere outside once again changed from balmy to rough. The wind howled as the rain battered the window in the dead of the night. They had arrived home just before the storm happened, escaping the torrential downpour spreading across the town. The cracking sound of thunder boomed, and lightning struck from the dark clouds, brightening up the sky for a second before vanishing.

Cristal's body lit up with pleasure as Daniel's kisses moved down her stomach. He was just a breath away from kissing her clit, and enjoying her womanhood below. Her mind whirled with delight.

For a moment, he tasted her pussy, lingering on her scent and pink lips with his tongue.

She moaned. Her nipples were hard as stones with the heat built up inside her. She could feel her juices leaking out of her and running down between her ass cheeks.

After Daniel had feasted between her legs, she angled her hips and gripped his ass tightly, her nails dug into his flesh. The sensation was authentic. Her legs came up and wrapped around his thighs, and she pushed him down. She wanted to feel him deep inside her.

He guided his erection near her. The moment his dick touched her pussy, Cristal felt a great heat rush through her. She moaned beneath him, her arms and legs tightened in a grip, and quivered from the dick thrusting in and out of her. Her pussy pulsed nonstop around his shaft. For a slim nerd, Daniel was packing eight inches and width.

Daniel set a slow and steady pace while inside of her, wanting the moment to last, while their mouths hungrily devoured each other's lips.

With the suction and her quivery heated velvet walls massaging his tool, Daniel moaned with throaty abandon as he thrust his dick all the way to her cervix. The pussy was too good. He felt his balls contract and release his seed deep into her.

Cristal's mind spiraled into a touch of bliss as her orgasm rocked her into screams for more.

Afterwards, Daniel held her in his thin arms, comforting her as the two immersed into some pillow talk. Cristal didn't want to leave anytime soon or have this moment stolen from her. She'd already lost so much, this little bit of happiness in her life was refreshing.

She closed her eyes, feeling Daniel's breath and his heartbeat against her, and exhaled.

SEVENTEEN

Since the shooting in the Bronx, Sharon was now on leave with pay, before being placed on light duty. In the papers, they called her a hero, and some called for her badge, calling her a murderer. The NYPD was still investigating the incident thoroughly, and everything looked to be in her favor. But, in reality, she knew that a white male in her same position wouldn't be under that long an investigation. As a matter of fact, it would be congratulations on a job well done, a child saved, and a thug dead—and most likely a promotion. She decided not to dwell on her job, and continued to focus on Pike's case.

It was another late night for Sharon in her dark apartment, seated at her desk near the living-room window, a modern table lamp on her right. The coffee she'd made earlier was already cold, and her eyes were heavy. It was three in the morning, and she was still going over a few witness statements from the day Pike was killed. She read each statement thoroughly, thinking the lead detective on the case could've missed something or investigated the case half-assed.

She assumed the NYPD viewed him as just another black male, most likely another drug dealer or gangbanger killed. Not even a blip on the radar.

There were about six witness statements saying they saw two or three black males wearing black and bandanas jump out of a maroon Chevy and kill Pike.

Meesha, Pike's ex, came across Sharon's mind. Did she have something to do with his murder? Everyone knew she and Pike had been feuding. Meesha wanted back in Pike's life, but he was dating Sharon. Did jealousy get Pike killed? Cops had questioned Meesha too, but she had a solid alibi, and there was no reason to suspect that she had set him up. Sharon wasn't going anywhere with the case, but she wasn't about to give up.

Two witnesses, one a crackhead, and the other a career criminal, in and out of prison multiple times, had both said in their statements that they got a good look at the occupants of the Chevy as it turned the corner, and they both swore it was two females inside the car wearing large sweat hoods. But, somehow, the detectives on the case convinced them that it couldn't have been two females, since too many other eyewitnesses said they saw two black males leaving the scene.

Something wasn't right with the case. It was back and forth. *Strange. Two men suddenly become two females from two witnesses' accounts.* Sharon had her suspicions about something or someone, but that thought was kind of far-fetched. Yet, anything was possible.

With dawn a few hours away, she decided it was time to get some sleep. She placed all the papers back into the manila folder, turned off the light on her desk, and went to bed. Tomorrow the groundwork would start. She would go out and talk to the witnesses herself.

•••

Sharon cruised through Harlem in her Fiat and came to a stop on the block where Pike was killed. She stepped out of her car under a graying sky and took a deep breath.

Going back to the scene where he was killed was always hard for her. She remembered that day so vividly. She remembered being somewhat incapacitated because she had been jumped by Meesha's crew, and Pike was there to have her back. It had started out to be a wonderful morning. He made her some tea, toast, and scrambled eggs, and was taking care of her. He had placed everything on a breakfast tray and served her breakfast in bed. He was going to pick up her prescription from the pharmacy.

Standing on the sidewalk, she peered up at the apartment they'd once shared. That day began to flood into her head again. She could see Pike getting dressed, ready to head to the store. He gave her a hug and kiss, donned his jacket, and the last words he ever said to her were, "Baby, I'll be right back."

She would never forget it. She could clearly hear him saying it, like he was standing right next to her. Then she remembered what happened right after he left—those dreadful gunshots ringing out.

Just thinking about it all over again brought tears to her eyes. She needed to take a deep breath and relax. It had been a few years now, but the pain was still fresh in her heart, especially with his case still open and the way she'd submerged herself in it.

She walked around the area, searching for one or two witnesses to talk to, if they were still around. She was willing to offer cash, ten or twenty dollars, to anyone who could point her in the right direction. She'd brought with her pictures of two young females, Tamar and Cristal. She had a gut feeling about something, but it was also hard to think her childhood friends could've had something to do with Pike's murder, but she couldn't escape the nagging feeling.

After an hour of walking, questioning people, and being relentless, she got what she needed. Sharon found one of the witnesses from that day, the crackhead Wilson, in a vacant apartment off Eighth Avenue.

Rochelle was lingering in a stairway, sitting there with a male friend. It was obvious they were about to get high. She looked like a bag of bones, her face sunken in like a skeleton, her stringy, unkempt hair a tangled mess.

Sharon interrupted their moment of bliss. "Rochelle Wilson, right?" she asked.

Rochelle became startled by Sharon's sudden presence in the dimmed stairway. She was ready to leave, thinking there was going to be trouble, and her male friend was about to do the same.

Sharon quickly identified herself. "I'm not here to

hurt or arrest you. Yes, I'm a cop, but I just want to ask you a few questions."

Rochelle and her friend looked unsure about what to do.

"It's about a crime you witnessed a few years back, here in Harlem. A young man was murdered," Sharon said.

"I don't remember no damn murder." Rochelle was fidgety and didn't look Sharon directly in her eyes.

"I'm sure you do. You gave your testimony to the detective."

The male sat quietly and timidly on the stairwell. He was frail-looking himself and far from a threat to Sharon. The only thing he seemed to care about was getting high.

Sharon stepped closer to Rochelle and said, "In your statement, you said you was sure that you got a good look at the occupants in the car, and you told the detective you swore it was two females in that car, not two men. You said they had on dark hoods. Can you elaborate more about that day?"

"Look, I don't remember anything about any murder."

"Just think."

Sharon pulled out the two small pictures of Tamar and Cristal and placed them directly in Rochelle's face. "Look at these two ladies clearly. Was one of them, or both, in that car that day?"

Rochelle went from looking edgy to agitated.

"The picture on the left, her name is Tamar. Does she look familiar to you? Could it have been her you saw that day? Just take your time and look at the damn picture!"

"Look, I can't remember anything about that day."

Sharon exclaimed again, "Look at the fuckin' picture, and just let me know—Do the one on the left look familiar to you?" She shoved the picture in the woman's face, almost coercing her to give the right answer.

"It could be the driver, but she don't look like her. It was too long ago, okay? I don't fuckin' remember her," Rochelle spat. "It wasn't her!"

"You need to fuckin' remember!" Sharon grabbed at the crackhead, clutching her clothing tight, almost slamming her into the wall.

"Get off me! Get off me!" Rochelle screamed. "Help! Help!"

The frail male took off running upstairs.

"Get off me! Please! I didn't do anything wrong. I don't remember. I don't remember."

Sharon came to her senses and released her taut grip from the woman's tattered clothing. What was she doing? It had happened again. She had lost control of herself.

•••

It wasn't the first time Sharon had badgered a witness. A few days earlier, she had gone to talk to a direct witness to the murder at her home. She'd found Cassandra McCollum's address and made an unannounced visit. She'd lived across the hall from Pike. She was a high-school senior at the time and so happened to be leaving the building lobby when Pike was killed. His death unfolded right before her eyes.

Sharon's girl-to-girl talk with the young woman escalated into a heated shouting match between them in the apartment. Cassandra said she saw two men in black, but Sharon tried to convince her that maybe it was two females dressed in black, to make it look like it was two males. But Cassandra was adamant about what she saw. She wasn't changing her mind, and it made Sharon upset.

Cassandra filed a complaint at Sharon's precinct, and she was given a warning.

•••

Sharon stepped away from Rochelle, looking at the woman apologetically. "I'm sorry," she said.

"Fuck you! This is police harassment!" she exclaimed, looking teary-eyed at Sharon.

"I'm sorry. I just have a lot of things on my mind."

"I'm gonna have your badge for this!"

Sharon didn't take her threat seriously, figuring that by the next time she got high, being drug-addicted, she would forget the whole thing. She pivoted away from the woman and exited the building.

The sky had gotten darker, like her mood. Things seemed to be going nowhere for her. She climbed into her car and sat behind the steering wheel for a moment. She thought about Pike. She always thought about him, every day. She missed him. She didn't want him to be forgotten.

She took a deep breath and said into the air, "I'm trying." She wiped away a few tears that fell from her eyes and started the car.

EIGHTEEN

●●●●●●●●●●●●●●●●●●●●●●●●●●●●●●●●

I t wasn't an issue of when she was going to kill Hector
Guzman, but how. Tamar debated with herself if it
should be done up close and personal—with a knife, a
razor, or her bare hands—or from afar, with a sniper rifle
possibly, or maybe poison. The thrill for her in taking out
a target up close, where her victims could see her face, was
the feeling that she'd snatched away their life. It brought
pleasure to her to watch them die; to see their lives slowly
vanish from their eyes.

She arrived in Santa Fe, New Mexico in the middle
of the afternoon. Santa Fe, the oldest capital city in the
United States, was getting ready for a lively festival called
the *Fiestas de Santa Fe*, an event held during the second
week of September, commemorating the re-conquest of
Santa Fe in 1692 by the Spanish after the Pueblo Revolt
of 1680. It brought many tourists into the city, giving
Tamar the perfect cover.

She arrived in Santa Fe after landing at Albuquerque
International Sunport on a midnight flight and renting a
car. From there, she drove Highway 550, an isolated and

barren thoroughfare. The stars in New Mexico looked so close, you could reach out and take one home with you.

It was her first time in New Mexico. Immediately, Tamar hated the place. Santa Fe was hot and desolate-looking. She was only there to do a job and didn't plan on staying long.

Hector Guzman was a drug lord who wanted to retire against his affiliate's wishes. The report on Hector was that he was a ruthless and coldblooded kingpin. He had smuggled billions of dollars' worth of cocaine, marijuana, and methamphetamines into the United States, and fought vicious turf wars with other Mexicans gangs.

Tens of thousands of people had been killed in the fighting, and many of his victims had been tortured, beheaded, and their bodies dumped in a public place or in mass graves. The violence had ravaged border cities and even beach resorts like Acapulco.

He was dangerous, unpredictable, and loved wild animals. His favorite animal was the tiger. He was known for raising a few Bengal tigers, which he would starve for days, and then for fun and cruelty, he would feed them by throwing his enemies and victims into the tiger pit. He enjoyed watching his animals viciously tear and shred men and women to pieces right before his eyes. It was his entertainment; he would sit and watch the carnage like it was a football game.

Now, Hector was a marked man, wanted dead by the same cartel he had helped build and had made rich. He'd fled from Mexico into New Mexico with twenty million of their cash and hoped to disappear. But Tamar was about to prove him wrong, and she wanted to make a spectacle out of it if she could.

She got to know his routine, his likes and dislikes. She'd done surveillance on where he laid his head, an impressive split-level Mediterranean home in Hacienda Santa Fe with five bedrooms and five bathrooms, remodeled with chiseled travertine floors, vaulted ceilings, a granite kitchen with breakfast bar and center island, a fireplace, a large pool, spa, and horses, along with an escape tunnel a mile long. The doors to the house were reinforced with steel, and surveillance cameras covered every square inch of the place.

She'd studied the blueprint to the home and remembered the layout from room to room. One mistake could cause her demise.

•••

The Fiestas de Santa Fe opened with a procession bearing a statue of the Blessed Virgin, known as *La Conquistadora*, to the St. Francis Cathedral. Tamar blended in with the crowd as she stalked her target. Hector Guzman was a short five foot six with a black moustache, wearing a cream shirt, dark jeans, and a cowboy hat.

The revelry started with the burning of Zozobra, also known as "Old Man Gloom," a huge effigy whose demise at the hands of a torch-bearing dancer symbolized the banishing of cares for the year. The event wasn't for the faint of heart and could be downright scary for children.

Hector, flanked by his armed men, was enjoying the evening like he was an average citizen of the city. He smiled and laughed, ate red ristras like they were crackers, and even flirted with a few beautiful young ladies.

Tamar cleverly followed him around the festival. She watched him and his men escort a few beautiful young ladies back into his armored SUV. There was no need to follow them, since she had already placed a tracker on the undercarriage of the SUV.

•••

Clad in a leopard Speedo, Hector Guzman put on a show for the three naked ladies that decorated his king-size bed. He was a hairy, shapeless man with a small gut, but the ladies didn't mind, because his money and power made him attractive. They drank expensive champagne and had three lines of cocaine on a glass mirror by the side of the bed.

One girl took a rolled up a hundred-dollar bill, put it to her nose, and did one long line without pausing.

The second girl went up to Hector with a teasing smile and kissed him on his stomach, while grabbing his crotch. She was ready to please him.

Hector cupped her B-size breasts and toyed with her nipples as she slid down his Speedo and didn't hesitate to take his small dick inside of her mouth.

"Yes, yes. Now this is my kind of party," he said.

She sucked him off, while the next girl went to help with the dick, sucking on his balls. The third, high off cocaine too, grabbed Hector from behind, ready to have sex with him and the other girls.

As the *ménage à quatre* was about to ensue, everyone in the room failed to realize that they had unexpected company in the bedroom. From in the shadows, Tamar, in a tight, all-black spandex suit, looked at the three sluts sucking off the drug lord's little dick with a blank gaze. In her hands were two black SIG Sauer P220Rs with silencers at the end of both barrels.

The girls pulled Hector onto the bed so that he was lying on his back while one straddled his chest and the other two whores continued sucking his little dick.

Tamar was ready to take him out. She wasn't worried about the guards. They'd all been killed—eight of his men, gone within the blink of an eye. The first two she took care of at the front entrance. One was shot in his eye, the second in the back of his neck.

Inside, she'd caught the next three swiftly in the living room. Three accurate shots into their foreheads, and before they could even blink, they dropped dead. She'd quickly moved behind the next guard and slit his throat while he was exiting a room. For the last two, she snuck behind one and put a long, sharp blade through his heart and gunned down the last man before he could react. Now Hector Guzman had no one to protect him, but his bitches.

Before the party got too heated, Tamar removed herself from the shadows of the bedroom and loomed into their sight. One of the girls screamed, seeing the female assassin in all-black with two guns in her hands.

Hector spun around, taken aback by her abrupt appearance. "What is this?"

Tamar looked at him with a cold, stoic expression.

"Such a beautiful little girl with big guns. You sure you know what you're doing with them toys? You know who I am? Let's not get hurt here," he said. "My men are all around this place."

"No, they're not," she said. "They have already been taken care of."

Hector suddenly looked spooked. "Who are you? Who sent you?"

"You already know about the mistake you made."

The bitches whimpered with fright as they looked on in horror at death waiting.

"I'm a rich man. I'll pay you triple what they're paying you. We can talk about this. You seem like a very rational person. I'm a man of my word."

She raised both of her guns in their direction, and the girls cried out.

Hector scowled, knowing what was about to come next. "Please, don't do this to me, not like this!" he shouted.

She opened fire.

Poot! Poot! Poot! Poot! Poot! Poot! Poot!

Blood splattered everywhere on the bed and in the room, but Hector Guzman was still alive. He didn't have a single hole in him.

Tamar had slaughtered all three ladies, leaving their bloody, naked bodies contorted on the king-size bed around him.

"I have a different arrangement for you," she told him.

"What's going on?"

She raised the gun to his head. "Let's go!"

"Like this?"

"Yes."

Hector slowly stood up from the bed. He no longer looked like a dangerous kingpin, but an aging man in bad underwear.

Tamar quickly restrained his wrists behind him with a zip tie and led him out of the bedroom. They walked past all eight of Hector's slaughtered men as she ushered him toward the front exit.

Outside, Tamar pushed Hector into the trunk of her rental car and locked him inside. The ignition started, and they went for a drive. She drove on the 502 for a short stretch and then took a dirt road right off the 502, where there was nothing but trees, hills, rocks, and dirt.

Twenty-five minutes later they finally came to a stop in a dark and isolated spot. Tamar killed the ignition and got out.

She opened the trunk and ordered Hector, still in his Speedo and his hands restrained from the zip tie, out of the car at gunpoint.

With her gun still on Hector, she led him deeper into the rough country, where there wasn't anyone around for miles. Hector couldn't help himself; he was panicking.

"My offer still stands," he said. "I can make you a very rich woman."

"I'm already a rich woman," she countered.

"There must be something you want."

"Yes, there is."

He turned to face her while being shoved forward, wanting to hear what she had to say. "Tell me and it's yours."

"I want you to die and for me to leave Santa Fe and head back home to New York," she said matter-of-factly.

They approached an area in the woods where the ground was disturbed and a large pit had been dug up. She marched him closer.

"Please, don't do this to me!" he shouted.

"Why not?"

"I'm begging you! Not like this! I don't want to die!" he exclaimed.

Tamar raised her gun and aimed it at him. No matter where he turned, his fate was sealed. He stood inches away from the pit, shivering.

"Either you jump in, or I'll shoot you and toss your body in." she said.

"No, no. Please, not like this!"

Tamar, sick of his whimpering and pathetic attempts to change her mind, aimed her pistol at his knee and fired. His kneecap exploded from the bullet ripping through it, and he stumbled backwards, falling into the pit.

Immediately, Tamar emptied her clip into him, silencing his pleas.

Now it was time to get back home. Melissa Chin still haunted Tamar, and she was at a complete loss as to how to find her.

NINETEEN

● ●

Tamar wasn't home for twenty-four hours when E.P. came storming into her apartment, scowling and looking like he was on the brink of a breakdown. He glared at Tamar. He didn't care that she'd completed the Hector Guzman contract smoothly. He was tired of hearing about her failures when it came to eliminating Melissa Chin.

"You dumb bitch!" he shouted, his eyes brimming with anger.

Tamar screamed back, "What do you want from me, E.P.? I fuckin' told you she disappeared, left a note behind, mocking us. Mocking me!"

"You're useless."

"I'm doing my fuckin' best!"

"Your best? You're nothing but a fuckup, bitch! I fuckin' made you!" he shouted. "I brought you into this organization, and this is the thanks I get. I assign you a simple task, and months go by while she still breathes."

"You find that bitch yourself!" she shouted.

"Don't fuck with me, cunt! I'll bury you where you stand. You always been useless!"

Tamar frowned at his comment. She clenched her fists and gazed at the kitchen knives behind him. Her bloodthirsty mind had her ready to thrust one of them into his chest.

E.P. stepped closer to Tamar, crowding her personal space and looking like a threat to her, his gun holstered under his jacket.

Tamar didn't draw back from him. She scowled too, knowing that the special thing they had with each other was dissolving.

"If Cristal was alive, she would have gotten it done," he said.

She was infuriated. She hated when E.P. brought her name up whenever Tamar failed at something. Tamar always felt second-rate to Cristal when it came to E.P. She was the rebound bitch—the bitch who did his dirty work. But he never respected her.

Tamar cursed him out, her mouth spewing venom and insults his way. When E.P. suddenly slapped her out of the blue, she didn't see it coming. She staggered from his blow and touched her bloody lip.

She rushed to grab a twelve-inch kitchen knife from the wooden knife block. She pointed the large knife at him with the urge to carve him up like a pumpkin on Halloween.

E.P. snatched the Glock from its holster and aimed it at her head. "Once again, you bring a knife to a gun fight."

They were suddenly propelled into a standoff, their eyes locked into each other.

"Don't be stupid, Tamar."

"I will fuckin' kill you where you stand," she said through clenched teeth.

Tamar's breathing was heavy. She once again felt that she was being set up. Something wasn't right.

Although she wanted to thrust the knife into E.P.'s heart and butcher him, Tamar knew she couldn't kill him. As a top associate in the Commission, he was off-limits. His murder would bring certain death upon her. But she was ready to protect herself if need be. She'd become quite skillful with knives over the years.

E.P. glared at her and the knife in her hand. He knew he had to control his emotions. Besides, he still needed her to track down Melissa Chin and kill her.

"Look, we're both getting out of control here," he said, lowering the gun from her head. "Let's me and you talk it out like grown adults."

"Talk about what?"

Though he lowered the gun, she continued to keep the knife lifted in his direction.

"I'm sorry that I put my hands on you. It was uncalled for," he said. "You know my temper. You're still my favorite." He smiled at her somewhat.

She didn't return the smile.

E.P. became cool, but Tamar didn't trust him. He was a conniving character and a slick talker. Despite his soft words, she could see in his eyes that he wanted her dead.

Tamar lowered the knife and kept her eyes on him. "So where do we go from here?"

"Back to business, like usual," he replied.

"Business?"

"Melissa Chin is still out there, right? She's still a threat, and they want her dead."

E.P. didn't have much more information on Melissa. It was still the same. Why was it so hard for him or the Commission to locate her? Why was there so little known about her?

Tamar put two and two together, and it dawned on her—Melissa Chin had to be an unsanctioned hit. That's why he knew so little about her. E.P. had been playing her all along. She didn't let on what she had figured out.

She started to question the hit she did on Cristal. *Did it come from the Commission, or did it come from E.P.?*

E.P. had her embroiled in his mess, and she didn't see any way out of it.

She started to think about her career with the Commission over the years. The money she'd made from killing had accumulated into seventeen million in an overseas account. She wanted to withdraw every dime of it and possibly make a run for it with her sisters and her little brother, the only people she cared about.

She thought about that plan, but in reality she knew it wouldn't work. She had two choices: She could either leave now without her money and disappear, or she could stay and try to fix the mess E.P. got her into.

Scared for her own life, Tamar plotted to get in contact with the Commission somehow and expose E.P. She wanted to clear her name and plead her case for mercy.

TWENTY

●●●●●●●●●●●●●●●●●●●●●●●●●●●●●●●●●●●●

Sharon walked into the captain's office with a calm demeanor, but she couldn't help being nervous. Being in the captain's office was like being in the principal's office.

"Shut my door," Captain Haymond said brashly.

Sharon did so and stepped into his office wearing civilian attire.

Captain Haymond, in a white shirt and black tie, with police insignias decorating his shirt, sat in his high-back leather chair behind his wraparound desk cluttered with photos of his family, paperwork, files, his computer, and other knickknacks. He gazed at Sharon impassively.

"Have a seat."

She took a seat directly in front of him

Captain Haymond was a burly white male with a military background. He had olive skin, cropped hair, deep blue eyes, and a dark mustache. He was stern but just. He locked eyes with Sharon, who remained silent, knowing to let the man speak first.

"You're a good cop, Sharon, and you have the bones to become a great cop."

Sharon smiled inwardly, but she knew there was more to come.

"You're off the hook for the Richard Jefferson shooting. Internal Affairs cleared it and deemed it to be a justified shooting. So you're back in. No more absence with pay or light duty. Congratulations," he said without a smile.

"Thank you, Captain Haymond."

"Don't thank me yet." He picked up a few sheets of paperwork from off his desk and tossed it her way.

Sharon's eyes shifted down to the white sheets covered in handwriting. She had her assumptions about what was on those sheets.

"You know what that is?" he asked.

"I have an idea."

"Those are three civilian complaints against you for this month alone, Officer Green. Three!"

"Who was the third complaint, sir?" she asked.

"Don't worry about who. You need to be worried about me."

"Yes, sir."

"Now listen to me and listen very closely and clearly. The Parnell Watkins case is now off-limits to you. Do you understand me?"

"But Captain—"

"Don't 'but Captain' me. All I want from you is a yes or no answer."

It was hard for Sharon to say yes. She felt she was so close to knowing something. Her gut told her two females had committed the murder. She even suspected that she might have known them.

"Answer me, Officer Green. Do you understand me? If you do not back off this case, then I will be forced to suspend you without pay this time, or worse, I'll have you back in uniform and directing traffic in the South Bronx."

"I understand. I'll back off."

"Wise choice," he said. "Now leave my office. And welcome back."

Sharon stood up and left immediately. The minute she was outside the captain's office, she wanted to scream out and punch something. She didn't want Pike to be forgotten, but she also needed her job.

She sighed heavily as she went into the locker room to relax for a moment. She went into the ladies' bathroom to splash her face with some water to wash away the tears trickling from her eyes. Pike's death would always disturb her, and she could never leave it alone or forget about it. She wanted to believe that there would be justice for his murder. His case couldn't end up like Biggie's or Tupac's. There had to be someone fighting for Pike, and she would be his warrior, even if it meant losing her job.

Sharon got her mind clear and herself ready to fight crime and arrest bad guys. She joined back up with her partner and hit the Bronx streets on a chilly, fall day.

"Welcome back," her partner, Brian Mauldin, said smiling.

"You miss me?"

"Like I miss an STD."

She laughed. "Yeah, you missed me."

•••

With Pike's case off-limits to her, Sharon started to concentrate on Cristal's case to keep busy with something while she was off-duty. Cristal was a good friend of hers, and the way she and her family were murdered was evil.

Using her computer savvy, she went through police file after file, going through encrypted information. She spent hours on her laptop in her home, reading every piece of information about her friend's case, going through photo after photo of the bodies in the apartment. She had grown close to Cristal's family over the years, from Grandmother Hattie to the cousins and aunts. It was hard to look at each gruesome photo and not tear up. It felt like her own family had been brutally murdered. She had to wipe away her tears, be strong and continue on. There was something evil out there, and she was determined to find out what it was. Tamar had proclaimed it was drug-related, but Sharon wasn't buying it.

As Sharon dug further, she found that the feds had taken over the case and started their own investigation. But there weren't any eyewitnesses like in Pike's case.

Sharon soon stumbled across some classified documents. There was also something strange about Cristal's case; like someone was hiding something. Sharon leaned back in her chair and sighed. Once again, it felt like she was getting nowhere. She wanted to dig further, but she didn't have any authorization. The feds were way over her pay grade. Her hands were tied.

She sat back in her chair and closed her eyes. It was after midnight, her apartment was quiet and still, and she had been at her laptop reading and looking at pictures for so long that her legs started to become numb. When she stood up to stretch, her legs felt like jelly. She plopped down on the sofa near her workstation and stretched out. Sharon needed to relax and take a quick breather. She was a hard worker and had always been, but she needed help. But who could she turn to?

She lingered on the sofa for a moment with her feet propped up on the end. Her eyes remained close, trying to brainstorm a name. Then out of nowhere she thought of someone. How could she forget about him? It had been so long since they had spoken or seen each other.

She jumped up and went to grab her cell phone from off her desk. She scrolled through the names until she came Domenic Swarthy. Seeing his name again made her smile and reminisce.

•••

They'd met after she graduated from the Police Academy. She had taken a trip to upstate New York for a few days before starting her new job as an NYPD police officer. Sharon was alone in Buffalo, New York, sightseeing Niagara Falls, enjoying some solitude. She had taken advantage of her time in Buffalo, walking across the Rainbow Bridge into Canada and viewing the three waterfalls.

Her modest vacation upstate provided a distraction from everything going on in her life. With Pike gone and Cristal too, it felt like New York City was trying to swallow her up with grief and pain. Sharon had graduated from the Academy with flying colors, but she had never been outside the city, and though Buffalo was still in the state of New York, being in a different atmosphere was fairly refreshing for her.

She met Domenic at a café one morning. She was waiting on line, while he was seated at a window table, reading the local paper. She was about to exit the café with her latte when Domenic stopped her to compliment her beauty and dark skin. He was a tall Italian man, six two, with breathtaking features and short, dirty-blonde hair. He had an infectious smile that radiated charm. His chest filled out his shirt, and his stomach was a washboard of abs.

Immediately, Sharon was attracted to him. They conversed all morning, getting to know each other respectfully, and by that evening, they were fucking each other's brains out in her hotel room. Domenic was the first man she had been with since Pike's death.

She remembered her legs spread open as his hips thrust forward, impaling her with his big dick. For a white, Italian man, he was blessed in size and width. She let out a grunt at the motion, her hands tensed into fists as her whole body went stiff as a board beneath him. They embraced tightly, grinding and pounding, humping, and grunting. Her body shook with a wave of pleasure that raced through her whole body. He was fully on top of her, gripping the back of her thighs, fucking her fervently in the missionary position.

When his mouth touched hers, a jolt of electricity passed between them. Her mind was awash with waves of lust as he was inside of her.

After their sexual rendezvous, Sharon learned he was a field agent with the FBI and had been with them for five years. They had a lot in common. They both came from rough neighborhoods and went into law enforcement because they felt it was their calling, and both had lost a loved one. Domenic had lost a younger brother to drugs, and his best friend to a car accident, and she told him about Pike.

After Niagara Falls, the two continued to see each other in the city. However, the affair was brief. He had a wife and kids, and had been married for eight years. After two months, she ended things between them.

•••

Sharon looked at Agent Swarthy's number and dialed it. She hoped it was the same number. She had no other way to contact him. The phone rang in her ear. She blew air out of her mouth and waited.

"Hello. Agent Swarthy speaking. Who's calling?"

Hearing his voice again made her smile, thinking about the fling they once had. But she kept it civilized and controlled her hormones, remembering he was a married man.

"Hey, Domenic. It's me, Officer Green."

"Sharon, it's good to hear from you again."

"Are you still in the city?"

"Nowhere else."

She didn't want to beat around the bush. "Can we meet?"

"Not a problem. When and where?"

"Is tomorrow good for you?"

"What time?"

"Noon."

"Yes, that works," he confirmed.

Sharon gave him the location, and they talked briefly. He inquired about her well-being and career, and she told him everything was okay.

...

Sharon walked into the Brooklyn park that sunny afternoon dressed a little better than usual in a white camisole top under a fall jacket and a pair of black coated high-waist jeans. Her heels strutted across the green grass as she walked toward the park bench where Domenic was already waiting for her, dressed in a dark suit and tie, looking like a federal agent. Most of all, he was still a very handsome man.

She smiled seeing him again, and he returned the smile.

"I'm glad you came," she greeted.

"Anything for you."

They hugged. She kissed him on his cheek. He smelled so good. She noticed he still had on his wedding ring. It didn't matter; they were only friends.

"You look good, Sharon," he said.

"And you too. What's it been? Three years now? I'm surprised your number is still the same."

"You know, nothing changes about me." He smiled. "So what brings me to the park on a warm day like today?"

"I need a favor from you."

"Shoot away."

Sharon handed him a manila folder as they sat on the park bench. "I need your resources for this case I've been looking into."

He opened the folder and leafed through the little pages inside. He examined a few pages quickly and said, "I see the FBI has taken over this case."

"The more reason why I need your help."

He didn't cringe when he saw the photos of the dead family sprawled across the apartment floor. He had seen worse. "They did a number on this family. Animals."

"The victims were friends of mine."

"I'm sorry for your loss."

"Thank you." She took a deep breath. "As you know, with this case handed over to the feds, my access to it is limited."

"And you need my reach."

"Yes."

"I'll see what I can do for you."

"I would appreciate it so much. I knew I could count on you."

Domenic closed the folder and looked at Sharon. They lingered on the park bench after talking. The way he looked at her, it was obvious he was still attracted to her. She gazed back, holding back her flirtatious behavior. She'd dressed for him, but she didn't want to take it any farther than the friendship that developed between them.

"You know, if I wasn't married, I would have definitely been with you."

She smiled. "It was fun while it lasted."

"And it could still last."

"I'm not a home-wrecker, Domenic," she replied respectfully.

"I know. It's one of the many reasons why I love and respect you. You're different."

Sharon stood up, ready to leave. "How soon can you do that for me?" she asked, changing the subject.

"Give me a week, tops."

"Okay. Bye."

"Bye, beautiful."

Sharon turned and walked away. Her wide smile hidden from his view, she could feel Domenic's eyes on her backside. She knew he was watching her walk away.

Domenic was right. If he wasn't a married man, they would've had a chance together. He wasn't Pike, but he sure came close.

TWENTY-ONE

* *

Sharon's cell phone rang while she was enjoying a soothing, warm bubble bath while listening to Chanté Moore and Kenny Lattimore. She jumped out of the tub dripping wet and snatched her cell phone from the sink counter. Seeing it was Domenic calling, she immediately answered the call.

"Hello?"

"Hey, did I call you at a bad time?"

"Oh, no, I'm just home, trying to relax," she said.

"I looked into the case and found out something major."

Sharon was listening intently, ready to hear what he had to say. She quickly toweled off with the cell phone to her ear. As she wrapped the towel around her wet, naked frame and knotted it near her chest, Domenic said to her, "Are you ready for this?"

"I'm more ready than ever."

"Your friend Cristal, she's alive."

Sharon thought she'd misheard him. *Did he just say Cristal is alive?* She was truly taken aback by the news.

She took a seat in her bedroom to keep from passing out.

"Alive?" she said in disbelief. "Are you serious?"

"Yes, alive. Your friend is, or was in the WITSEC Program. She was the lone survivor of the home invasion."

The pill he was giving her was so big, it was almost too hard to swallow.

"The feds were ready to prosecute a Mexican drug kingpin named Hector Guzman. Mr. Guzman had been supplying her boyfriend for years. His name was Hugo, a top guy on the food chain. The agency suspected that things went sour between Hugo and Mr. Guzman, and they decided to massacre the entire family. Somehow, your friend became tied up in their mess. Cristal was supposed to testify against the Mexican Cartel, but right before the trial, she disappeared. It's believed she left on her own free will, slipped away from the WITSEC Program in the middle of the night. And, get this, they found Hector Guzman dead in New Mexico a few nights ago—someone fed him to some hungry tigers. He was torn apart."

"Ohmygod!"

"To my knowledge, the agency isn't using any more resources to find and keep her safe. They can't force her to live under their umbrella. Hector Guzman was the least of your friend's problems. If the cartel catches up to her, they will most certainly finish what they started. The only good news is, no one knows where she is. She just vanished into thin air."

Sharon's mouth was wide open. Cristal was alive. She still couldn't believe it. It was great news, but weird news.

"Whatever your friend was into, Sharon, it turned into a shitstorm, and people are dying left and right."

Sharon sighed heavily. It felt like a ton of bricks had landed on her shoulders. Maybe Tamar was right. She really didn't know Cristal. The information her friend had given her screamed drug-related for sure.

"Thanks, Domenic. I appreciate what you did for me."

"No problem. If you need anything else, don't hesitate to give me a call."

"I won't."

After they both hung up, Sharon lingered on her bed for a moment, thinking and worrying. Cristal was all she could think about. *If she's alive, then where would she go?* She had to find her. And she had to reach Tamar again, to tell her the good news that Cristal was alive.

TWENTY-TWO

●●●●●●●●●●●●●●●●●●●●●●●●●●●●●●●●

Cristal stood butt-naked in her living room in Boston staring at her bedroom wall. She frowned, her fists clenched, as she looked hypnotically at the images in front of her. She had death and revenge on her mind. She gazed at her past and her foe in front of her, reminiscing about only the bad that had happened to her. Displayed on her bedroom wall were blown-up pictures taken last week of Tamar, her mother Black Earth, and Tamar's three siblings, Jada, Jayson, and Lena. Cristal had been watching them and learning their moves and their schedules. She had become their shadow—lurking and thirsty to react.

She'd witnessed everything from a distance, taking photos of everything that moved and whoever was related to Tamar. The pictures she took that hurt the most were of Tamar and E.P. together. Cristal wondered if E.P. knew Tamar and some goons who murdered her family.

Was her best friend also fucking E.P. the whole time while she was with him, and that's why she came to kill her? Was it about jealousy? It was obvious they were having sex. She had the proof.

Was E.P. also involved with her family's murder? Did the Commission even sanction the hit on her? There were so many questions swirling around in her head that she couldn't reconcile.

There was no way Tamar could take everything away from Cristal and be allowed to live. Revenge was inevitable. Cristal was just biding her time, watching and plotting. This dish would be served cold, and it was about to get wintry cold soon.

Originally she was waiting for Tamar's twenty-fifth birthday, when the Commission allowed her to age out. Tamar would have had millions waiting for her right before Cristal took her life. But now Cristal knew it was all a lie; there was no aging out. She could speed up Tamar's death.

Every day, Cristal wrestled with the idea of whether or not she should kill Tamar's little siblings, knowing they were the only people Tamar ever cared about. She pondered making them suffer in front of Tamar's eyes, the way she'd watched her own family suffer. It would have been a pleasure to see the look on Tamar's face as they were murdered.

Cristal shed a few tears as she hooked her look on the children's pictures. She wanted to make everyone pay. Yet she remembered that Tamar's sisters and little brother were like her own siblings. They were close, like a family. Jada and Lena looked up to her, and Jayson followed her around like a lost puppy.

Before Cristal met Daniel, there wouldn't have been

any hesitation on her part; Tamar's family would have been dead. She had thought about making all five of them scream out for God's mercy as she brutally snatched away their lives. Now that she had been swamped, almost brainwashed, with his positive outlook on life, she'd been thinking about going easy on the kids and only making Tamar and Black Earth suffer.

She missed Daniel dearly and couldn't wait to be back in his arms again. She'd spent three weeks with him and then left again. It was hard to leave North Carolina. She had a life there—a simple life, and a good one. But her reality once again came calling. She had an objective that needed to be completed. She told Daniel she was leaving for Africa again and she wasn't sure how long she'd be away this time.

He believed her. He didn't want her to go, but he understood. The night before she left, they made passionate love and had heated sex.

Cristal had been back in Boston for two weeks and thought about Daniel every single day. She was in love with him, but nothing was going to stop her from implementing her revenge on Tamar. They all had to die, even E.P. It was no longer about business; it was definitely personal.

TWENTY-THREE

●●●●●●●●●●●●●●●●●●●●●●●●●●●●●●●●

I t won't be me," Tamar said to herself. She wasn't going out without a bang.

Tamar took a few drags from the cigarette burning in her hand and blew out the smoke. She sat parked a comfortable distance from E.P.'s Westside penthouse apartment on 78th Street in a dark blue Maxima, something standard and low-key, a loaded .9mm Beretta on the passenger seat. She had been stalking him for the past week, watching his comings and goings. Her every movement had to be subtle—a different car for a different day—since E.P. was trained to observe any irregularities.

If she fucked up, it was certain death for her. So she sat silently and vigilantly behind the steering wheel.

She wanted to get a handle on the Commission. She had been killing for them for years and never got a glimpse of the people in charge, their identities highly protected. Everything was through indirect contact, either through a third party or a message from an anonymous sender. Tamar figured E.P. would provide the best lead to finding and meeting with the Commission.

She took a drag from her cigarette and flicked it out the window. As she did so, E.P. came walking out of the lobby, alone and well dressed in a pea coat and wingtip shoes. Tamar eyed him from several cars away as he walked toward his burgundy Bugatti Veyron.

As he pulled off, she did the same, following three cars behind him. It was late evening, and traffic in the city was heavy. Tamar didn't want to lose him, but she also didn't want to give herself away. Men like E.P. were trained to pick up a tail. Her driving had to be ingenious. One mistake and one of two things could happen—he would spot her, or she would lose him.

The one good thing about following E.P. was the car he was driving. Being high-end and exotic, it was easy to spot on the road.

They headed south on Riverside Drive and transitioned into West Side Highway. Traffic was decent on the West Side, and so far, she'd been able to follow him without being conspicuous.

From the West Side Highway, she followed him into Lower Manhattan, passing the Freedom Tower being constructed. It was a magnificent sight, and a long way from Ground Zero. The tower was New York at its finest.

Tamar didn't get too patriotic. She kept her sights on the back of E.P.'s Bugatti, watching his brake lights and keeping a safe distance. The traffic grew a little thicker going toward Whitehall Street, deep in the heart of downtown Manhattan. She remained four cars behind him and kept her cool. She switched lanes and spotted the rear end of his car. He was crawling behind a box truck, and cars were rubbernecking because of a fender bender on the side of the street.

Tamar left her rental on the street in a tow area and followed E.P. onto the ferry that was soon departing for Staten Island. Being rush hour, the ferry was almost at capacity, carrying close to 3,500 passengers and forty vehicles.

Keeping her head low and her eyes discreetly fixed on E.P., she watched him move around on the top deck near the back of the ferry, as he faced Manhattan and kept to himself. She had to keep her distance—one look her way and he'd be sure to spot her.

As the ferry traveled toward Staten Island, giving the riders aboard a breathtaking view of the Manhattan skyline and Lady Liberty, Tamar continued to blend in with the crowd. A few wide-eyed tourists stood around with their digital cameras and cell phones pointed at a variety of the city's attractions, while the regulars calmly made their way home from work.

Tamar watched E.P. sit down next to a man on one of the open seats on the deck. She couldn't fully make him out, but he was Caucasian, dressed nondescriptly, and reading the newspaper.

Who is he? Is it a coincidence that E.P. so happened to sit next to him?

She situated herself closer to the two of them, keeping out of their view, using her surroundings to camouflage her presence. The crowd definitely gave her an advantage. She made small talk with a smiling married couple in matching Dallas Cowboys jerseys. It was obvious they were from Texas, with their country accents. She volunteered to take a photo of the two while passing the Statue of Liberty. As she entwined with them, she continued to watch E.P. from her peripheral vision. He was still seated next to the man. There didn't appear to be any communication between them, but her gut feeling told her they were up to something.

"Thank ya, so much," the wife said to Tamar.

"You're welcome," Tamar said, playing nice. "First time in New York?"

"Yes, it is," the wife replied.

"You'll love it here."

"I already do," the woman replied, looking too affable.

Tamar excused herself from the couple.

For the duration of the ride to Staten Island, E.P. sat next to the man, and then as the ferry was about to dock at St. George Terminal on Staten Island, he suddenly stood up and walked away, while the man remained seated, reading the newspaper. Something was odd.

She couldn't get a good look at him. By the time she tried to see his complete face, the ferry had docked, and everyone started to hurry toward the exit. A crowd came between them, and she lost sight of him. She felt confident she was on the right track. She lit a cigarette and caught the next ferry back to the city.

On different days of the week, around the same time, Tamar would follow E.P. to the Staten Island Ferry and once again watch him sit next to the same nondescript man for a moment before the two went their separate ways. She was sure the man meeting with E.P. discreetly would bring her closer to the Commission and allow her to clear her name.

•••

Tamar sat in the large tub, simmering in the heated water, sipping on expensive champagne, trying to relax from her troubles. Near her reach was a loaded and already cocked .9mm, just in case some unwanted company came charging into the bathroom. The lavish hotel room she decided to stay in was decorated with plush fabrics and neutral tones and equipped with wireless Internet, an en suite bathroom, and a huge wall-mounted flat-screen TV.

Believing security at her place was compromised, she'd checked into a room in New Jersey under an alias. She destroyed anything connected to her. The only thing she had was her cell phone. It was a risk to keep it, but there was information she needed on it, and it was the only way her siblings could contact her. But she planned on getting a disposable cell phone soon as possible.

Tamar lingered in the tub for an hour. Her situation with E.P. was on the verge of a meltdown. It was either her or him. She felt she was being set up. So every movement had to be a chess move.

She thought about the man on the ferry. How high on the food chain was he? Was he the main guy? And why was E.P. meeting with him? Was it about her? There were so many questions, but no one to answer them for her. She expected to get an answer soon, though.

She removed herself from the tub and toweled off. Then she picked up her .9mm and inspected it. It was fully loaded with a few hollow tips. The gun was clean; no bodies on it. She had more guns in the other room. She was heavily armed and ready for anything that came her way. It wasn't hard to leave her apartment and her life behind. In the world she lived in, lingering on anything could get her killed. Walking away from anything, even her family, in thirty seconds flat was her key to survival.

She went into the bedroom and sat on the bed. Still in her towel, she removed a few devices from her bag and placed them on her bed. Tamar had her apartment rigged with miniature pinhole surveillance and motion cameras, all linked to her smart phone. She logged in, entered a pass code, and her apartment appeared on the small screen. She checked each room, and everything looked still.

She closed out the app and went over to the window. From the fifth floor, New Jersey was a dreadful-looking place in her eyes, with a view of the Turnpike, industrial buildings, and a few factories. The area of Jersey she was in was cramped with traffic and pollution.

Tamar closed her blinds, darkening the room even more. She picked up the remote and powered on the TV then sat at the foot of the bed to take in the evening news.

As she placed her gun under the pillows about to get ready for bed, her cell phone rang. She picked it up from the nightstand and looked to see who was calling. The number was unfamiliar, but she answered anyway. "Speak," she said quickly.

"Tamar, it's me, Sharon."

Tamar thought she wouldn't hear from Sharon again. Her call was a surprise. "What do you want?" she asked, being gruff.

"We need to talk," Sharon said. "It's important."

"About what?"

"Not over the phone. Can we meet somewhere?"

Tamar was skeptical. She had a lot going on at the moment. Meeting with Sharon wasn't her priority, but the urgency in her tone suggested it was something really big. "Tomorrow," she said.

"Where?"

"The park where we used to hang out at."

"I'll be there." Sharon hung up.

Tamar couldn't sleep. She lay in the bed staring up at the ceiling, her gun underneath the fluffy white pillows. The television was on mute, but her mind was blaring.

TWENTY-FOUR

● ●

Sharon walked toward the basketball courts in the East New York park. It was early afternoon, and the park was still empty. On this desolate fall afternoon, there was no children's laughter or sweaty men playing pick-up games on the court.

She gazed at the basketball court and thought of Pike. She and her friends would sit around for hours watching him dominate other players on the court. An All-Star player and a showboat, he could dribble, pass, shoot, and dunk. He was NBA potential, but he'd made a few bad choices in his life that ended his chance to play pro ball. She smiled at the sweet memory of Pike jumping into her head.

Ten minutes later, Tamar pulled up in her flashy Beamer and stepped out looking like a diva. She strutted Sharon's way clad in a St. Laurent leather biker jacket and a pair of spiked heels, looking like trouble. She stared Sharon's way, unsmiling.

They met by the park bench near the basketball court. No one else was around.

Tamar said, "This was our park."

"It definitely was. You miss it?"

"Sometimes."

Tamar got straight to the point. "What you call me out here for? I know it ain't to talk about the past. That shit is gone and forgotten."

Sharon locked eyes with Tamar and came out with it. "Cristal is alive."

"That's fuckin' funny, Sharon. I don't have time for fuckin' games with you."

"I'm serious. She's alive. She's still out there somewhere. I have a friend in the FBI, and he confirmed it."

"What?"

"I know it's hard to believe, but she survived that night. She was the only survivor."

All the color drained from Tamar's face. "How?"

"Cristal's always been a tough girl. You know that."

Tamar refused to believe the bitch was alive. She'd personally put four bullets into her, two in the head, and watched her die. She'd watched everyone die. She felt like she was in an episode of *The Twilight Zone*.

"Your friend in the FBI, do they have her whereabouts?" Tamar asked, reaching for some kind of information.

"Her whereabouts are unknown, but she's out there, Tamar," Sharon said excitedly. "She's alive, and she can shed some light to everything that's been going on."

Tamar kept her cool and pretended to be excited about the news too. "This feels like a dream," she said. But

Tamar was far from excited about the news. Cristal being alive fucked everything up.

"I'm going to find her."

"So no clue on where she is, huh?"

"She disappeared from the WITSEC Program a while back. She was to testify against a drug kingpin, a Hector Guzman. But he ended up dead."

"This friend in the FBI, you have his name?" Tamar asked out of the blue.

Sharon raised an eyebrow. "Why do you need to know his name?"

"I'm anxious to find her too. If she's alive, then we need to find her and make sure she's okay."

"She could be anywhere, Tamar."

"So where do we start?"

"I don't know," Sharon said. "But I will know."

Sharon's strong attitude toward finding Cristal worried Tamar. Not only did she have to fear the Commission finding out that she'd carried unsanctioned murders, but she didn't successfully take out the target, Cristal. Now the local police and feds were involved. But her biggest fear was Cristal. She was out there somewhere. The threat of Cristal popping up anywhere was unnerving.

But then something else became immediately clear to Tamar—Melissa Chin had to be Cristal. *Fuckin' bitch is snitching out our life story.* She knew what Cristal was doing, and she had to put a stop to it.

Tamar looked at Sharon with a change of attitude and said, "If she pops up, give me a call."

Tamar pivoted and walked away, leaving Sharon standing there with a questioning stare at her former friend.

As Tamar walked back to her car, Sharon shouted, "That's all you have to say?"

"After all this time, you tell me she's alive? I have to see it to believe it," Tamar replied, not even bothering to turn back around.

Tamar didn't have time to stand there with Sharon and talk about a ghost. Shit just became critical for her. She needed to get to the Commission and fast. Now her life was on the line, and the threat was coming from different directions. She climbed into her Beamer, turned over the ignition, and peeled out of her parking spot, tires screeching and all that.

TWENTY-FIVE

●●●●●●●●●●●●●●●●●●●●●●●●●●●●●●●●

The explosion was so loud, Cristal felt like the ground beneath her feet was about to cave into a massive hole and swallow her up. She was shook up from the blast. The air around her was suddenly dense and toxic with billowing black smoke that could be seen for fifty miles. And the heat was intense. It felt like hell was all around her, and the devil was tapping her on her shoulder. Coughing erratically, Cristal couldn't breathe, and the darkness was sucking the life out of her.

Then there was another loud explosion. And then another. Dynamite was perpetually exploding like fireworks on the Fourth of July.

Wherever Cristal turned or tried to run, she was cut off and trapped into an unnatural black cloud of smoke that formed a ring around her. She fell to her knees in agony. But the pain had only just started. She looked ahead, but the thick black smoke made it so she couldn't even see her own hands.

Then she heard voices, their loud screams piercing her ears. From the smoke emerged a dark silhouette, the eyes cut out, but the grim-looking face recognizable. Cristal's mouth gaped open as the dark apparition came her way.

Grandmother Hattie's body reached out to Cristal, and her scorching touch seared into her flesh. Another face emerged from the dark smoke—this time it was her Aunt Ruth, and she also grabbed Cristal with a fiery hold that made her feel like her skin was on fire.

Her cousins came next. But her unborn child haunted her most. Each damned soul plunged their claws into Cristal, and she screamed like a banshee. They'd all come back from the dead to blame her for their deaths.

She stretched out her arms until they couldn't stretch any longer, reaching out to some invisible support and trying not to be pulled under. "No! No! Please, get off me! I'm sorry! I'm sorry!" she yelled out.

Suddenly, she felt someone grab her as she flailed around in the bed, screaming out hysterically.

Daniel reached out for Cristal and pulled her into his arms. "It's okay, baby. It's okay," he said in a soothing tone.

He cradled Cristal in his arms and held her gently. She couldn't stop shaking and was sweating profusely. The nightmare felt too real.

"It was only a bad dream," he said, holding her affectionately. "I got you, baby. I got you."

Daniel turned on the lamp on the nightstand. Cristal was still shivering. He kissed her tenderly and said, "I'm here, Bee. I'm here for you. I will always be here for you."

With her head pressed against his chest, she could hear his heartbeat thumping. She closed her eyes and listened. His voice was in her ear, his touch was reassuring, and his hold was strengthening.

"I got you, baby. Everything is going to be okay," he declared with certainty in his voice. "I promise."

Her chest heaved rapidly with heavy panting. Her breathing was still ragged. Her lips trembled with each outlet of air, the intake fluttering as it struggled to infiltrate her constricted throat and feed the heaving lungs and palpitating heart.

"Just breathe easy, baby, easy," Daniel whispered in her ear. He massaged her chest, cooling her nerves bit by bit.

An hour later, Cristal fell asleep with Daniel by her side, spooning against her. She didn't know what she would do without him. She had been back in North Carolina for two days, and every moment with him was an encouraging one.

•••

Cristal woke up alone in bed to the smell of breakfast permeating the air and the morning sun percolating through the open window. She swung her feet over the side of the bed and planted them against the parquet flooring. She stood up and stretched. The sunlight filtering through the window suggested it was going to be another beautiful fall day in North Carolina.

"Grandma Hattie," she uttered out of the blue. She could hardly remember the nightmare, but it spooked her a great deal.

She donned one of Daniel's T-shirts and went to join her man in the kitchen. He was by the stove frying something up. She could hear the grease popping in the pan. It smelled like bacon.

Daniel stood over the stove with his back to her, his body bare of any tattoos. He was one of a kind.

He turned around to see Cristal looking his way. A smile immediately splashed across his face. "Good morning, beautiful."

Cristal stepped farther into the kitchen. She felt embarrassed about last night. She hated for Daniel to see her like that. "I'm sorry about last night."

"There's no reason to apologize. It was simply a bad dream. We all have them."

Daniel had no idea about her past. His world was simple; trying to get through med school, paying bills, and living a humble life. She didn't want to pull him into her nightmares. He didn't deserve it. So, she kept him apart from who she really was. She had to. Cristal felt she was protecting him from the demons that haunted her. She didn't want them haunting him too.

Daniel went to her and wrapped his arms around her. He hugged her and planted a kiss on her lips. "I love you."

"I love you too."

"Breakfast is almost ready."

"What you cooking?"

"Bacon and eggs, and some salmon croquettes, something my mother taught me how to cook," he said with delight.

She smiled. "Sounds good."

"You're going to love it."

Daniel turned and attended to the stove again. His kitchen was coming to life with a sweet aroma.

Cristal sat at the kitchen table and watched him work. He was special. "Look at you, trying to become Bobby Flay," she joked.

He laughed. "Hey, I try."

"Yes, you do, and you're the best, baby."

"I'm glad you feel so."

They looked at each other with expressions of pure love. Daniel loved her, scars and all. Cristal didn't feel ugly around him. She didn't feel the need to cover up the keloid on her face or put on any makeup. Daniel liked her just the way she was. But she remembered what she used to look like.

"I have a surprise for you," he said.

"You do?"

He nodded his head. "Something special."

"Tell me," Cristal faintly begged.

"No, it wouldn't be a surprise if I told you right now."

"Not fair."

Daniel laughed.

He served her breakfast at the table. Everything looked delicious. The salmon croquettes looked extra tasty. They were a golden, fried brown and already had her mouth watering.

"It looks good," she said.

"Wait until you try them."

She picked up her fork and dug into the salmon. Her taste buds exploded. "Damn! This is really good, Daniel."

"I'm glad you like it."

"I love them. Wow!" She stuck another piece of salmon into her mouth. "Mmmm ... now this is breakfast."

Daniel couldn't stop grinning. He joined her at the table, and they shared a wonderful breakfast together, devouring every piece of food Daniel cooked. Breakfast was so good, Cristal felt like licking the plate.

•••

Before Cristal knew it, the day had gone by, and it was late evening. Their day together was blissful and simple: first, shopping at the nearest supermarket, and then a walk in the park. Then she helped him tend to a few things in the house that needed fixing.

As the day turned into dusk, the couple shed their clothing and shared a bubble bath. The mood was set with Daniel placing rose petals in the bath and romantic music playing. He started out the bath with a toast for two from champagne chilling in a bucket nearby.

At first, they agreed not to speak to each other for the first half-hour, communicating instead by touch and emotion. They used a bath sponge to wash each other. He treated his partner as if she was royalty, spoiling her, gently giving her a sensual massage in the tub.

Cristal snuggled next to him and lay against his chest.

"I hate it when you leave, Beatrice, especially for such a long periods of time. I'm miserable without you. And I worry about you."

Cristal released a deep sigh. It was upsetting to her, knowing she'd lied to him about her real name.

"You okay?" he asked.

The soothing bath, his loving words, his touch had her feeling vulnerable. She felt terrible about it all and was tempted to reveal the truth to him, but she kept her lie strong.

"I'm okay," she said. "What time is your first class tomorrow?"

"Eight in the morning."

"Well, let's not waste any more time then," she said, turning herself over to face him in the tub, her breasts pressed against his thin chest, and began to kiss him fervently.

They used extremely soft towels to dry each other off when they were done bathing. Then they blow-dried and brushed each other's hair. They completed their special evening by having a plate of romantic finger foods and downing more glasses of cheap, store-bought champagne.

In the heat of the moment, Daniel sheathed on a latex condom, pushed Cristal's upper body slightly forward, and found her wet entrance from behind. The entire night went on like that—making love, drinking champagne, and pillow-talking until they both slept peacefully.

"You never did tell me what my surprise was."

"It's coming," he hissed against her ear.

• • •

Daniel and Cristal enjoyed a nice multicourse dinner in a romantic setting. The lounge, with spectacular city views overlooking the river, served a delicious dinner buffet and offered an array of creative cocktails. After dinner, they took a long carriage ride to a high peak out of town, where they could take a moonlight stroll and enjoy a star-filled sky.

It was the perfect setting. Their love was going strong and speeding in the fast lane. Cuddled together, the world felt different for Cristal.

Daniel kissed her cheek. "Remember that surprise I told you about the other day?"

"Yes, I remember."

Daniel gazed at her as the carriage ride was about to come to an end. The look in his eyes said that he only wanted to be with her and only her. Then out of nowhere came the ring box. He slightly got down on one knee and revealed the 1/7-carat diamond hearts ring in sterling silver.

"Beatrice, will you marry me?"

Cristal was floored. "M-marriage?" she said, stammering.

"Yes. I love you. And I want to spend the rest of my life with you."

She didn't know what to say. She was stuck. She couldn't say yes to him, but she didn't want to break his heart.

Daniel was still on one knee. "We can build something together, you and I, baby."

"Daniel, I need time to think," she replied quietly.

"Think?" Daniel looked baffled by her comment. "Don't you love me?"

"I do; more than anything. But I'll be leaving soon."

"I know. It's the reason why I want us to get married. I'll be finished with school soon. I know times are rough now, but it'll get better."

Cristal still was unsure. He was still calling her Beatrice and believed that she was in the Peace Corps, aiding and helping poor people around the world. How far could she carry the lie?

Their carriage ride came to an end, and Cristal still didn't have an answer for him. Daniel looked a little disheartened.

When they stepped off the carriage, she said to him, "Look, I'm not saying no, baby. All I'm saying is, let me come back from overseas, and I'll give you my answer then. I'm not going anywhere, Daniel. I love you." She already knew her answer. It couldn't be.

"Okay. I understand."

They kissed on the street.

Daniel hugged her close. Every time she was in his arms, he always gave her the feeling that he never wanted to let her go. Her biggest concern was, her layers would peel right before him and he would see her for who she truly was. She never wanted the way he looked at her to change.

TWENTY-SIX

●●●●●●●●●●●●●●●●●●●●●●●●●●●●●●●●●●●●

Autumn in Martha's Vineyard was the best time of the year. The humidity had left, the beaches were free of summer tourists, and the trees were starting to turn into the most beautiful shades of red, yellow, and orange.

Crusty brown leaves whirled around in a circle in the front yard of The Bishop's cottage. The mystifying colors of the sun shone onto the pile of leaves as the scent of the ocean blew over Cristal's shoulders and neck, giving her a tingling sensation.

It was the season of hoodie sweatshirts, early evening walks, pumpkins, apple pies, and driving around with the windows down.

Cristal couldn't get Daniel's proposal out of her mind. She needed to get away to think. And the best place for that was at The Bishop's cottage.

The Bishop was in the back room of his cottage painting again. He sat in front of his canvas, barefoot and shirtless in a pair of jeans . Cristal stood behind him, watching him paint and listening to him talk.

"Painting is quite simple once you follow some fundamental tips," he said to her.

The portrait, a forest in the fall with a flowing river, was coming alive. The Bishop had a good eye for art. As usual, he had his opera playing and was sipping on a glass of wine.

He continued his lecture. "A painting is made up of different elements that come together to make the work what it is. You ever wonder why painting is so comforting and exciting? The colors, the fluidity of the paint, just the experience of creating something on a flat surface right before your eyes . . . it's like telling a story." He gently touched up the leaves of a yellow birch tree, bringing out the red and yellow of autumn. "It is as if the paint has a personality, and it becomes a person. Someone who can talk to you and express what you keep deep inside your mind and your spirit."

He made sense to Cristal. But he always made sense to her.

"It's like the paint, the brush, and the canvas all collaborate to create their own story," Cristal said.

The Bishop turned and looked at her. "Well said."

She smiled.

"He asked me to marry him," she blurted out.

"Who? Your boyfriend in North Carolina?"

"Yes."

He continued painting. "How do you feel about him?"

"I love him."

"You love him," he repeated.

"Yes. But this life we live, what we do, how do I make it work? He's an innocent, a civilian."

"Do you remember what I told you about finding your niche? Well, if he's your niche—"

"But I'm lying to him, Bishop. He thinks I'm Beatrice and that I travel the world working with the Peace Corps to help with the needy."

He turned around in his chair and grinned at Cristal. "I'm Sam. Remember that."

He stood up, finished painting for the day. He walked toward Cristal and stood close to her. Locking eyes with her, he said, "Do you remember what I said to you before about how to survive? It's not just about killing and being dangerous; it's about being able to fit in. It's about maintaining a balance of work and life."

Cristal nodded.

He placed his hands on her shoulders, and she could feel his strength.

"Beatrice—that's a lovely name for a lovely woman who's doing a pleasant thing, helping people. And your life with Daniel allowed that to be your niche. He never needs to know about Cristal. He fell in love with Beatrice, and so it is. That's who you become. The transition doesn't have to be difficult."

The Bishop made lying sound so easy.

"Killing people has to be the first priority, but it doesn't have to be your only priority. Just be careful. If you love him and he loves you, then that's your life."

She nodded again. It was easy to attain a fake

passport, driver's license, social security number, and birth certificate. She had her connections. But could it be so simple for her? Could she fully become Beatrice? She had enough money saved, but she wasn't ready to retire, not yet. She still had unfinished business to take care of.

"Now, if you can excuse me, I need to wash up," The Bishop said.

He walked by her and undressed while on his way to the bathroom. Cristal caught a glimpse of his buttocks, and for an old man, he still had it going on.

Cristal walked outside and breathed in the cool fall air around her. She had a lot to think about.

TWENTY-SEVEN

T amar was disguised in a long wig and characterless clothing as she rode the Staten Island Ferry at 6 p.m. sharp. The ferry was teeming with riders and tourists, as usual. It was a breezy, autumn day with a feeling of gentleness on the boat. People were chatting and laughing. The view of the Manhattan skyline was always breathtaking, but she wasn't on the boat to take in the view or chat with anyone. She was trying to save her life.

She tried not to worry about Cristal being alive. If their paths crossed, then she would be ready. She planned on taking care of her problems before her problems took care of her.

From a short distance, with dozens of people obscuring her view of the man, she kept a keen eye on him, observing him seated at the rear of the ferry as was customary. He was an aging white male, sharply dressed in an expensive gray suit with manicured fingernails, and salt-and-pepper hair. He had an air of power about him.

Tamar moved closer his way, lightly pushing her way through the thick crowd of riders on the boat and taking a seat across from him, where she had an angled view of him. She watched another man, another operative, take a seat next to him. They both pulled out the day's newspapers, blocking their faces, and it seemed obvious they were in communication with each other. She wished she could hear what they were saying.

She continued to watch him closely, trying to get to know everything about him. The wind from off the water picked up, blowing her wig into her face. She hooked her hair behind her ear. Strapped with her .9mm in her handbag and blending in with the others, she remained patient.

Twenty minutes later, the ferry docked at the St. George station in Staten Island. At once, both men stood up and separated. Tamar stood up to leave too, trying to be tactful and cunning with her movement, watching the man's back as it moved through the tight crowd of passengers heading toward the ferry exit. People spilled out of the station onto the street. Tamar moved quickly but cautiously, trying not to blow her cover or let him out of her sight.

As she followed behind him, she noticed a black Mercedes E-Class with tinted windows idling outside the ferry station, with a man standing by the passenger door. It was clear he was waiting on someone.

Tamar quickly took in his appearance, well dressed in an Italian suit, tall and serious-looking. He had a brawny physique behind the clothes. He could be the driver or pure muscle. She could tell from the bulge in his suit jacket that he had a holstered weapon.

As predicted, the man on the ferry went toward the E-Class, folding the paper in half and placing it underneath his arm as he strode toward the car with a sense of urgency. The driver in the Italian suit promptly opened the back passenger door, and the man slid into the backseat. The door was quickly shut after his entry. The driver slid behind the wheel, looking methodical.

Tamar had a split second. The wheels turned right, and the Benz started to drive away. She got close enough to the car to remember the plate number.

Next time, she would be ready.

•••

The next day, it was the same routine, but this time, instead of traveling by ferry into Staten Island, she crossed over the Verrazano Bridge onto the island and made her way toward the ferry station. She sat idling outside the St. George station, and as predicted, she observed the E-Class Benz drive up ten minutes before the 6 p.m. ferry was to dock.

She kept her gun close and her nerves cool. Whoever this guy was, she needed to talk to him somehow. How she was going to do it, she had no idea, but she had to get his attention.

The driver waited.

She waited.

Around 6:15 p.m., the ferry docked, and moments later, hordes of people started to spill out from the station and onto the street or on the waiting buses on the bus platform.

Tamar's mystery man came walking on schedule, newspaper folded and underneath his arm. He walked toward the Benz and climbed into the backseat. The door shut, and his driver got behind the wheel and drove off.

Tamar followed them south to Bay Street then onto Victory Boulevard. The sun was slowly setting, rush hour was still at its peak, and traffic started to stall as they got nearer to the Highway 278. She made sure to be cautious, always several cars behind them, trying to predict their movement on the street. They passed the Silver Lake Golf Course, still on Victory Boulevard, where it was one lane going in both directions.

The Benz made a sudden U-turn, spinning around on the narrow street, nearly hitting a parked car, and headed her way.

Tamar fixed her eyes on the car; she was stopped behind a minivan at a stop sign, and the Benz was approaching fast. Her instincts told her to take out her gun.

The driver's window rolled down, as the car raced her way. His outstretched arm came out the window, and a Glock 17 came into view.

Bak! Bak! Bak! Bak! Bak! Bak!

Tamar quickly crouched down in her seat.

Her windows exploded, and shards of glass landed on her. She scurried toward the passenger side, gun in hand, hastily pushed open the door, retreated from the car, and spun around already aiming at the fleeing Benz. She had the car dead on sight. She opened fire, but to no avail. The car was moving fast and vanished.

"Fuck!" she cursed loudly. She couldn't give chase. The driver had shot out two of her tires, leaving her stranded on the street.

The sudden shootout created unwanted attention. Eyes were everywhere. And soon, the police would show up. Tamar couldn't linger around the scene because they might come back for her with a hit squad.

She abandoned the car, scaling the chain link fence and running through the cemetery. She could already hear the police sirens blaring.

Tamar knew one thing for sure—he was either part of the Commission, or connected to it in a major way.

•••

Tamar had to lie in hiding for a couple of weeks. She lingered in different hotel rooms week after week, using different aliases. Her every movement had to be calculated, even when going out for food. She felt like a fugitive on the run. She didn't know who to trust or who to go to. The shootout didn't spook her; she was built like a rock, but she had to be smart.

She remained tenacious about getting in contact with the unknown man always riding the ferry into Staten Island. *Think, Tamar, think,* she thought to herself. *Why is he always on that boat a certain time? Was it a setup?* She wasn't sure who was watching who. Was she watching them, or were they watching her? She had to think straight, put two and two together.

She was gazing out the window of her room, from the eighth floor, an assortment of guns and high-velocity rifles displayed on the bed. She wasn't planning on taking any chances. Her attention was fixed on dozens of civilians below, people coming and going, their lives so simplistic and one-dimensional. So, how did her life become so complicated? Death could be waiting around the corner if she wasn't extra careful.

Her cell phone rang. It was E.P. calling. He was always calling. She would ignore most of his calls. She didn't trust him at all. He would text her, asking about her condition and her location. Did he think she was a stupid bitch? She would simply text back: Still hunting for Melissa Chin, and oh, btw, Cristal is still alive!!!

When E.P. found out Cristal was still alive, he thought it was a lie. He continued to blow up Tamar's phone demanding more information from her—How did she know she was alive? Who told her?

She looked at his incoming call and said to herself, "Let the muthafucka sweat. Fuck him!"

What she was doing was simply biding her time on meeting back up with the Commission, and that unknown stranger was the key. This time she wouldn't make the same mistake following him.

Missing her siblings, she decided to give them a call. It was always good to hear their voices. She hadn't seen them in weeks. She missed taking them shopping and then out to eat. But she had to stay away, with Cristal lurking and her enemies emerging from the woodwork.

Jada's cell phone rang a few times. Finally, she picked up, her young voice on the other end sounding so innocent. "Hello?"

"Hey, little grown woman," Tamar answered, always calling her little sister that.

"Tamar, where you been at?" Jada said, lively and excited.

"I've been busy. I got a lot going on."

"When are you coming by again? It's been really hard here with Black Earth since you been gone," Jada said, her voice changing into some sadness.

"I'll be back to visit all of y'all when I get the chance and things cool over. How are Jayson and Lena?"

"They're fine. They're missing you too."

"You sound so grown, Jada."

"I started high school this year," she said.

"You like your school?"

"Yeah, it's cool."

"You got a boyfriend yet?"

Her little sister chuckled. "No, no boyfriend," she said shyly.

Tamar chuckled. Her little sister was fourteen years old. Her only brother, Jayson, was now twelve, and the baby of them all, Lena, was nine.

"I had my first boyfriend when I was ten."

"You did?"

"Yup. His name was Randy, and he was eleven years old. *Illll!* I still can't believe I liked him like that," Tamar said humorously.

Jada laughed.

"Where are Jayson and Lena?"

"Not here, outside playing."

"Tell them I said hello when you see them, okay?"

"I will."

"I love you, little sister."

"I love you too."

"And I promise I'll be there to see y'all soon and take y'all shopping and have our day out like we used to, okay?"

"I know, Tamar."

Tamar teared up a little. Jada was a sweetheart, and Tamar hoped she grew up to be a doctor, lawyer, or businesswoman. She wanted her siblings to make something out of their lives. The path she chose, it was her choice and she felt there was no other way for her. Killing people, in a way, provided a better life for her sisters and brother.

Unbeknownst to them, Tamar had set up a trust fund with $50,000 in each of their names, for school or business, theirs on their twenty-first birthday. It was the least she could do for them.

"Everything else is okay, Jada? No problems in school or home?"

"No, everything's cool. I can take care of myself."

Tamar smiled. "I know you can. You got my blood in you."

But if her sister did have a problem with anyone, Tamar wouldn't hesitate to eliminate the threat.

They talked for a moment, and then it was time for Tamar to hang up.

"I love you, little grown woman," Tamar said from the bottom of her heart.

"I love you too, Tamar. Hurry up and come see us. We miss you."

"I will. I promise."

Tamar hung up with a heavy heart. She sat at the foot of the bed and picked up a pistol. She had to make some changes quick.

•••

Tamar took a drag from the Newport and then flicked it into the waters. Once again, she was back on the ferry and observing the unknown stranger seated in the area like always. It was evening and the graying sky above was overcast. The weather was chilly with Halloween nearing. She kept out in the open and watched everything around her with a vigilant eye. She was extremely nervous, but remained watchful and ready.

Under the black ladies' trench coat she wore was a concealed Glock 19 and a few daggers for her protection. She eyed the man from her position, took a deep breath, and made her move. It was now or never.

She took a seat directly next to him, and didn't say a word at first. The man didn't even flinch. He kept cool, not acknowledging her at all. It was like she wasn't even there.

She knew another associate was about to take the same seat, but it was her only chance.

Tamar opened up her own newspaper, emulating the movements of the previous men who had sat next to him. "I need to talk to you," she said to him.

He kept quiet and still like a statue, his eyes reading the newspaper.

"I know who you are," she quickly spoke, "and I think you know who I am too. I'm not here to hurt or threaten you. I just want to talk, simple as that."

Still, there was no response from him. Silence.

It was frustrating her that he wasn't saying anything back or trying to acknowledge her. She had to get his attention somehow.

"She's alive," she said. "Cristal. She's alive. I have critical information about her. She and E.P., they were having an affair. My source told me that Cristal was in witness protection. She was going to testify against a Hector Guzman, a drug kingpin I killed a few weeks back. Now that's a twist of fate."

Then she said, "E.P. can't be trusted."

The ferry sailed by Governors Island. Everything seemed cool, and nothing appeared out of the ordinary.

"I can be an important factor to the Commission. I know I fucked up," Tamar continued. "I can find her, Cristal. She's been spreading my business and the Commission's business in a series of books. The pen name she uses is Melissa Chin. I won't make the same mistakes again."

The man started to close his newspaper, evenly placed it underneath his arms, simply said, "I'll look into it," and stood up. He still didn't give Tamar any eye contact. It was as if he was a machine.

Tamar stood up too.

What just happened? She said to herself. *Did it work?*

They started to go their separate ways. He'd made it clear that he didn't need to hear any more. As the unknown man walked away from the seating area, he gave a slight head nod to the machinist on the ferry.

The emotionless machinist, dressed like a blue-collar worker, sent the text.

Tamar took three steps away from the area and her head suddenly exploded from an assassin's bullet ripping through her skull and spewing her blood on a woman's face and a man's jacket.

She dropped like a sack of potatoes.

At first, it seemed unreal to the occupants on the ferry. But as the body lay sprawled out on the deck of the ferry, a woman shrieked from the horror unfolding in front of her.

The shot was fired from a building on Governors Island over 1,700 meters away, despite the wind velocity and the crowd of people around her. The marksman was already packing up his equipment and making his escape.

The ferry transitioned into panic as Tamar's body lay dead in a pool of blood, her brains exposed to the overcast light.

Calmly, the unknown man and the machinist removed themselves from the area.

TWENTY-EIGHT

● ●

The black Yukon lurched as it quickly turned onto a dirt road toward the obscure location a hundred miles outside of the city. Overhead, the woods closed in, shutting out the moonlight. The SUV came to the top of a slope, where the trees thinned. There was a deep little dell, and beyond that, an abandoned cabin barely standing in the boondocks, surrounded by miles and miles of trees.

The vehicle came to a stop. Already parked in the area was a black Lexus. Two men in dark suits climbed out of the Yukon and went toward the back. They lifted the hatch and roughly removed a man who was tied by his wrists and gagged. He had been badly beaten.

They carried E.P. inside the cabin, where a third man waited, and threw him to the floor. He landed on his side with a thump against the dusty flooring.

E.P. quickly got up on his knees and was surrounded by his captors, all three glaring down at him. The bruises on his face were fresh. His suit was dirty and torn. He looked defeated.

"What the fuck you want from me?" he growled.

"Just to talk, E.P., that's all," the alpha of the three said.

"I don't know shit!" E.P. shouted.

"I bet you do. It's just gonna take a little a convincing on our end."

The alpha male had tousled dark brown hair, thick and lustrous, his eyes a mesmerizing, deep ocean-blue, his face strong and defined, his features molded from granite. He was dressed impeccably in a dark blue Perry Ellis three-piece suit.

He stepped closer to E.P. and crouched near him. He fixed his sharp eyes on E.P.'s battered face. "You and I, we do go a long way back, don't we?" he said.

E.P. glared at him. "Fuck you!"

The man chuckled. "Your girlfriend is dead," the man said.

"Fuck that bitch!"

"Yeah, I know you did . . . and had a great time with her too. What about Cristal? How is she?"

E.P. had no words for him. He scowled with his jaw rooting and clenched his fist. Burning rage hissed through his body like deathly poison.

Phlegm dripping from his nose, E.P. spat in the man's face.

The man stood up and said to his armed goons, "Hang this muthafucka up!"

They grabbed E.P. off the floor and dragged him to the back of the cabin. They strung him up by his arms to a pole with rusty shackles attached to the ceiling, his arms above his head, fully outstretched, his feet tied below. They stripped him of his clothing, leaving him only in his boxers.

The man, out of his suit jacket, shirt and tie, had donned a long smock. He had on a pair of gloves and a sharp, small knife in his hand.

"You know what flaying is, E.P.?" the man asked.

E.P. squirmed and became feisty. "Fuck you!" he shouted.

The man laughed again, slowly circling E.P., mocking him.

"A thousand years ago, they used flaying as a method of execution for witches, war prisoners, criminals, people like that," he said, placing the small knife against E.P.'s cheek. "They would hang the person up by the wrists and start peeling the skin from the face, and then all the way down to the feet, until all the skin was off."

E.P. squirmed and wriggled in his restraints, not caring for the history lesson at all.

"Now, in most cases, the victims died before the torturer even got to the waist," he continued. He held the blade against E.P.'s skin and slowly moved it down his frame, almost pushing the tip of the knife into his rib cage.

The man speaking in a well-mannered tone was known to a select few as Z. He was a brutal and sadistic killer, and known to be the Commission's favorite hit man and torturer. He had cruel methods of making people talk.

E.P. grunted.

"Okay, shall we begin?"

Z placed the knife against E.P.'s face again and twisted the blade into his right cheek, peeling back a piece of his flesh like he was peeling a potato.

E.P. screamed, "Aaaaaaaaahhhh!"

"Yes. Scream for me. Scream."

Z picked sections of his face to carve up. His warm blood oozed from his wounds. His pain was an icy wind choking the breath from his lungs, and it came like a sudden squall out at sea.

E.P.'s breathing became ragged. His face became grotesque from the flaying. As the life bit by bit drained out of him in its garish red, his remaining skin took on the pallor of a corpse.

When there were no more sections to flay from his face, Z started to work on the body—his chest, his nipples, his ribs, and his abs and started to peel away slowly.

E.P.'s screams echoed out loudly, piercing the air like a siren. His blood flowed like a lazy river. He started to talk, giving them some information on the Cristal Clique and why he'd had Cristal killed.

After an hour of flaying, Z had everything he needed from E.P. No one had ever lasted this long, down to the waist.

"Kill me," E.P. said faintly, his body looking like bloody lunch meat.

Z looked at him. He was ready to grant E.P. his wish. He reached his hand out, and one of the goons placed a .45 in it.

"It's been fun, E.P. But everything must come to

an end," *Z* said, placing the barrel of the gun to E.P.'s forehead.

E.P.'s eyes fluttered from the pain, and his body was on fire everywhere. Blackness filled the edges of his vision, and the only thing he could hear was his own fading heartbeat. He yearned for death.

Poot!

E.P.'s body lay slumped in its restraints, his blood dripping onto the floor like a leaky faucet.

"Who's hungry?" *Z* asked.

His men looked at him; it wasn't anything new to them.

The men had everything they needed. Next, the Commission planned on doing some extensive investigating using all their connected contacts.

In the end, they put it together: Melissa Chin was Cristal. She was a threat to their organization, and she was now working for their rival, GHOST Protocol. She had to die.

But it was complicated. A meeting had to be arranged. An approval needed to be met.

TWENTY-NINE

* *

ALBANY, NEW YORK

The sleek, luxurious Rolls-Royce Phantom pulled up to the check-in area of the Hilton Hotel in the heart of the Capital District. The car came to a stop at the entrance, and the chauffeur quickly climbed out of the Phantom to assist his passenger with his exit. He opened the back passenger door and stepped aside.

Stepping out of the car was a well-dressed man in a $7,000 Brioni suit, clutching a Doyoner walking cane. Alfred Whitlock. His hair was gray, and so was his trimmed goatee. He had an aura of supremacy and mystique to him. He gazed up at the hotel and said to his driver, "Don't park the car far," and proceeded toward the hotel entrance alone.

Ten minutes after Whitlock's arrival, a pearl-white Rolls-Royce Ghost pulled up to the hotel entrance. Stepping out of the back was a tall white male with thick jet-black hair, piercing blue eyes, and high cheekbones.

Jacque Colin was dressed sharply in Armani, and looked intense and powerful, like the head of a Fortune 500 company. He walked into the hotel, also alone.

Fifteen minutes later, a silver Maybach arrived at the same hotel, and exiting the exotic chariot was a white male in his late sixties, Carlton Birdwell, dressed flawlessly in Tom Ford with diamond cufflinks glimmering and a gold Rolex peeking out from his white shirt.

The last and final vehicle to arrive was a classic Benz with the black rag-top. It stopped and stepping out was another aging white male dressed in a Jay Kos suit, face wrinkling with his thin hair and hard eyes. Harold Perricone. He walked forward.

It was the Commission; four very wealthy aging white men who were pillars in their community. The Hilton hotel was a neutral location. A secret meeting had been arranged with GHOST Protocol to discuss a very important matter.

All four men walked into windowless secured conference room on the first floor, capable of seating twenty people. Already waiting were members of GHOST Protocol. The door had been locked, and each man took a seat at the fourteen-inch racetrack conference table and leaned back in the high-backed leather chairs.

They all looked like executives and businessmen—which they were—but they were also leaders of organizations that had people killed.

At the head of the table was GHOST Protocol's top man, Villa Wellington, a tall, bearded black man dressed

Steve Harvey-sharp, standing six foot two and weighing three hundred pounds, with intense eyes and a cigarette-raspy voice. He exuded confidence.

Also associated with GHOST Protocol were two other well-dressed African-American men, pillars of their communities—multimillionaires with thriving businesses and degrees from Harvard and Yale, but murder for hire was a much more profitable enterprise.

Anthony Black and Timothy Greenwood were middle-aged men, ex-Marines once turned mercenaries then turned businessmen. They had founded GHOST Protocol twenty-five years ago.

Seated silently and straight-faced beside Villa was The Bishop. Dressed in a black Alexander Amosu suit, his presence alone was intimidating. He was quiet and looked each man in the eyes as they sat before his superior.

"Gentlemen, welcome," Villa greeted, standing in front of everyone, his height and size towering over the table.

"Let's get to this business," Jacque announced. "I have other affairs to attend to."

"And we will."

The Commission was there to discuss implementing a green light to have Cristal assassinated. The Bishop felt uneasy about her demise being discussed, but he kept quiet and still, like a servant inside the room.

"This Cristal, from our understanding, she now works for your organization," Carlton said. "And she has become a problem and a liability to our organization."

"She's running her damn mouth! She's writing stories, telling things that do not need to be told. She's gone rogue! Can you even control this bitch?" Alfred Whitlock chimed.

The Bishop clenched his jaw, but he kept his cool. It wasn't his place to speak.

Villa sat back in his seat and leaned back into the chair. The Commission had his undivided attention. He clasped his hands together, glanced at Anthony and Timothy, and remained silent, allowing the men to voice their concerns to him.

Jacque said, "As you know, our two organizations have worked in parallel with each other for years now, and we aren't looking to create any conflict. In respect, we've reached out to your organization to correct this problem."

"Her being alive is also a threat to GHOST Protocol," Carlton said.

"How's that?" Black asked.

Alfred slid one of Cristal's best sellers in Villa's direction. Villa picked up the thick book and leafed through it silently to the parts highlighted by Alfred.

"She is Melissa Chin," Jacque said. "She needs to be silenced."

"She's only writing about the Commission," The Bishop said, finally breaking his silence, hearing enough. "This is no concern to us."

Alfred asked, "And how soon will she betray GHOST Protocol with her words aimed at your organization, spilling your secrets and the way your network works?"

"Your network is a cesspool," The Bishop said gruffly. "Murdering their own recruits, lying to them and stealing what is theirs—what kind of organization is that?"

"The inner workings of their organization are irrelevant to us, Bishop," Villa interjected evenly. "The only matter before us is Cristal's fate."

The Bishop frowned. If he could, he would have ripped all four men apart with his bare hands.

"I can foresee this being a problem for us in the future," Timothy Greenwood said.

Anthony slightly nodded, agreeing with Timothy's statement.

The Bishop knew he was losing. His associates were going to vote against him. He leaned back in his seat and continued to frown.

"Then we must put this to a vote," Villa said.

Villa looked at Anthony, who instantly gave the green light.

He then looked at Timothy, and his vote was the same.

He looked at Bishop, and Bishop quickly said, "I vote no."

Villa also agreed to green light the hit on Cristal, so The Bishop was overruled three to one. "It is done then," Villa said.

The men on the Commission smiled.

"There has to be another way," The Bishop exclaimed.

"The only way is for her to die," Timothy said. "The decision is final."

"Then I'll do it," The Bishop said. "Let me be the one to take her out. She knows me, and she won't even see it coming." In his mind, he would do the hit mercifully, whereas the Commission would undoubtedly torture her.

Villa looked his way seriously and said, "You have one week to make it happen."

The Bishop nodded.

THIRTY

●●●●●●●●●●●●●●●●●●●●●●●●●●●●●●●●●●●●●●●

Cristal had heard about Tamar's murder right away via the news. She knew the Commission was behind it, her brains blown out by a sniper's bullet on a crowded ferry. It took extreme skills to execute that contract. The puzzling question for her was, why did they want her dead? What did she do to trigger her demise? Cristal didn't know what to think.

Who would be the Commission's next target? Would they come after her next? Did they even know she was still alive? She tried to keep herself cool, but nothing made sense. Now it was chaos.

She sat at the kitchen table cleaning her arsenal. Each gun had to work to perfection. She couldn't afford to have any weapons jamming up on her at a time like this.

It had been two weeks since she'd seen Daniel. She missed him a lot. She thought about his marriage proposal and was still unsure if she should say yes or no. The Bishop's advice was insightful, but her mind was still clouded.

Daniel thought she was in Uganda this time, overseeing a food drop into a war-torn country. The lies continued, and his trust for her had grown stronger. He couldn't call her, and she didn't call him. She thought about him every single day and couldn't wait to be in his arms again. But before she could go see him, she had to get a few things in order.

Each gun and rifle was thoroughly cleaned, outside and in. She placed her arsenal in a safe spot and stepped out onto her balcony clad in a robe.

It was a chilly November day. The crisp copper leaves were falling off the trees swaying gently in the fall wind, the clouds above overlapping each other, making the sky a gloomy gray. She stood on the balcony for a while, watching the city of Boston come alive with activity and traffic.

Alerted by the sound of her water boiling in the teapot, she went back inside. As she poured the steaming hot water into a coffee cup, she suddenly thought, *I'm the last one standing. Mona, Lisa, and Tamar, they're all dead.*

Sharon was never in the game, so it was safe to say that her future was brighter than all of theirs. A quick sadness came over her, but it was brief. She didn't have time to grieve or reflect on the past.

Sipping on her hot tea, Cristal sat at her desk, her laptop open. On screen was the next chapter to her fourth book. She only had one-third of the story written. It was flowing. She arched over her laptop and allowed her fingers to stroke the keyboard, typing herself into a different world. She wrote about her involvement with E.P. and Hugo.

I stood gazing in the mirror at my disarrayed hair after the wild sexual episode I'd experienced with P.T., and it made me want to cry. I was drowning in guilt.

P.T. had ravaged my body throughout the night. He did things to me, worked his thumb up my ass as I started using my muscles to coax out another load of cum. He would smack my ass, fucking me doggy-style and pulling my long hair, then reaching around to grab my tits and cup them tightly. His behavior in the bedroom was freakish, but it turned me on. He was rough with my nipples, pinching them, squeezing them, and making me moan with a deep howl.

Afterwards, the guilt overcame me. I was messing around with two men, but Mason was the one I loved. How could I go back home to Mason after what P.T. did to my body? I was trained by the Syndicate to become whoever I needed to be to get the job done, but this time, I couldn't come up with the right lie.

P.T. walked into the bathroom naked. His rock-hard body glistened with sweat, and his muscles flexed as he came up behind me. He pulled me into his arms and held me tight. It felt like I was wrapped up in his personal cocoon of lust and sex.

Once again, he proclaimed his love for me, sending my fault and shame into a cyclone of emotions. We were two killers in heat. It had to be one of the most dangerous episodes in the bedroom, with his firearm shooting off my orgasm into a fiery craze.

"You okay?" he asked me.

"Yes," I said. "I just have a lot on my mind."

"What is it?" He sounded genuinely concerned for my well-being.

"It's nothing."

I couldn't tell him I was in love with another man. I wanted to put an end to my affair with him. It was a dangerous liaison.

But on the flip side, I was benefiting so much by fucking P.T. My affair with him brought me closer to the Syndicate. Sex with him had its perks. I was rising to the top, becoming one of the few femme fatales in the Syndicate. Why rock the boat now? I knew I had things under control, and as long as P.T. was happy, he would never find out about Mason.

Cristal stopped writing for a moment, feeling a little nostalgic. She took another sip of tea and heaved a sigh. She stood up for a moment and walked to her window.

Though it was after midnight, she wasn't tired. She still had a lot more writing she wanted to do. Inside, she felt like a dam that was ready to burst open. The next chapter she started on was the heaviest and most painful to write.

She sat back at her laptop, determined to tell one of the roughest parts of her life. It had to be told.

After the slaughter of my family, I was surprised to see that I was still alive. Why? Was it an unwanted gift or a curse thrown upon me?

I felt blackness all around me. I could feel and smell the death of my family. I could hear the voices of the EMT workers trying to revive me. This was the nightmare I couldn't wake up from. It was stuck on me like my own skin.

As the EMT wheeled me out of the apartment, I heard myself uttering in a panicky voice, "My baby!"

"Ma'am, you've been shot four times," the male said to me. "We need you to relax and get you to a hospital. You're alive!"

He'd said it as if he was surprised that I was still alive.

How did this happen? Tandi! I wondered what her price for her betrayal was and why she had to go after my family. She exclaimed before shooting me at point-blank range that I'd broken the rules. So why did my family have to suffer too?

Before I got to the hospital, I lost consciousness.

**

I awakened from my coma, losing sense of everything around me. I didn't know the date or the year, or how I had ended up in the hospital. But I was angry. I felt paralyzed by fear and grief, and then despair.

It didn't take long for me to fall into depression. It was an unseen, unheard, silent killer. I couldn't escape the feeling of guilt no matter how hard I tried. The depression followed me around like a black shadow on the inside, eating me apart and waiting for me to die.

I stood on the brink of something dreadful. The heaviness of everything seemed to press down on my shoulders. I struggled to take even a single step forward. The memories of my family being slaughtered flooding my brain was too much. It kept coming and coming, deeper and deeper. I sank under a sea of rage. It was too much. All of it.

But I somehow kept it moving. I couldn't give up, but every step taken cost me. The darkness grew darker, and my pain grew sharper; it all seemed to only grow in strength. I began to wonder if it would ever get better.

What kept me alive was pure hatred and rage. It was the thirst for revenge on those that I had trusted. But the life I chose was a constant nightmare that had no end or happiness.

Cristal stopped typing and sighed deeply, the pain of that day etched in her mind. She was transfixed by her words on the screen. The words came easily because the pain never went away.

This chapter in her life—how would that end? Would it end with Daniel and her, happily married? It all seemed too farfetched for her. Could killers like her drift away into some fairytale land to live happily ever after being marked by hell? When would the day come when a sniper's bullet took her out?

She stood up from her desk and walked back out onto the balcony. Her fists clamped around the railing, her mind drifting into emptiness. She closed and eyes and simply stood there.

Her cell phone chimed. She turned but didn't rush to answer the phone. She entered the apartment and picked up. The caller ID was unknown. She answered anyway. On the other end, a familiar voice was able to snap her out of her gloomy thinking.

"I need to see you," The Bishop said.

"How soon?"

"Leave now," he said.

"I'm on my way."

Hanging up, Cristal immediately started to get dressed. His tone sounded uncertain about something. She knew there was something wrong. She threw on her jeans and running shoes, loaded a few pistols into her handbag, and walked out the door.

THIRTY-ONE

T he Bishop sat in his still cottage feeling uneasy about the contract on Cristal. He couldn't talk anyone out of it. It was sealed. They wanted her dead within a week, and it was already going on day two. He'd never had any problems carrying out any contracts in the past. Over the years, whoever they said kill, he killed. No hesitation and no regret on his part. His victims were just contracts—almost like business deals.

He sat in the dark, shirtless, and in a pair of cargo shorts, the Desert Eagle with the suppressor around the barrel in his hand.

He'd called Cristal over two hours ago. She was about two and a half hours away. He wasn't in any rush to kill her.

He was still conflicted with the choice, though. She was like a daughter to him. He didn't have kids. It was his one mistake.

But his loyalty was to GHOST Protocol. He was allowed to live a cushy life, retired in a way, but calling the shots behind the doors; assigning murders instead of doing them.

How should I go about this? he asked himself.

He was ready to make it clean and painless for Cristal. She would come inside, in the dark, he would then take her out from the shadows, a bullet to the back of her head. She wouldn't even see it coming. He had done it plenty of times before. He could dispose of the body himself or call a cleaner to handle it.

As he waited for Cristal's arrival, he was flooded with memories of her. She was someone to talk to, someone he had grown close to. She loved his paintings, and she was one of the best killers he'd ever seen. Her mistake was her literature. Writing about what they had done and how they'd done it was a death wish. He had one of her books with him but chose not to read it.

He was against her writing about hit men, political corruption, and secret agencies, almost like a Tom Clancy novel. But it was understandable to him. He had his artwork and she had her writing.

The Bishop, seated in complete silence, waited for over three hours and then he heard the cab pulling up to his place. He stood up and walked toward the window, peeping through his blinds. He saw Cristal get out of the cab and pay the driver before coming his way.

A deep breath came out of him.

He could hear her coming up the short steps and looming closer to the front door. Gun still in his hand, he waited calmly. The front door opened up, and she walked inside. He had her dead in sight—one bullet and it was over with.

Cristal turned around and locked eyes with The Bishop. She saw the gun and didn't flinch. "They sent you, huh?" she said calmly.

He didn't say anything, the Desert Eagle aimed at her head.

Cristal stared at him and simply waited for the *bang!* But it never came.

He lowered the gun. He couldn't find it in his cold heart to kill her.

"They green-lit your murder. You have less than a week to disappear," he told her.

She wasn't shocked to hear it.

The Bishop walked farther into the living room and reached for her novel placed in the chair. He tossed it at her and said, "No more stories."

She didn't say anything.

"The Commission met with GHOST Protocol, and they will hunt you down and kill you. It was an unfortunate tragedy, what happened to your family. That was an unsanctioned hit. The man responsible for is dead. But they still want you dead."

"And go where?"

"Far from here, Cristal. It is no longer safe for you, probably, nowhere in this country."

"But Daniel—"

"The contract is for *your* life only, not his. He'll be fine."

"But what about you, Bishop, when your agency finds out that you didn't fulfill the contract?"

"Don't worry about me. I can take care of myself. It's my decision. I can live with it. But you need to leave right now."

The Bishop went into another room, and Cristal followed behind him. He pulled open a dresser drawer in the bedroom and removed a small bag. Now was the beginning of her vanishing point.

"You'll need a new passport. Destroy every passport the agency gave you. You won't be able to use them."

He handed her a disposable cell phone and a phone number. "I have an outside connect for you that you can trust. Everything and everyone else will be compromised. You do not trust anyone. Understand? No one! Assume that everyone is a threat to you."

Cristal nodded.

The Bishop went on to counsel her on what to do.

"When you leave town, don't go to any place you've talked about or stated a desire to visit. Don't run to any place predictable. Don't hide in a city or town you've been to, or where you're known to have family. The agencies are smart; they're trained to track people anywhere, and they have access to surveillance cameras, people, things, law enforcement. Don't underestimate these people."

The Bishop moved around his cottage hastily, gathering more items for her.

"And most important, stay away from Mexico," he stated. "They have informants and agents scattered all through Mexico. It's easy to drive into that country, and everyone heads there if they have a bounty on their heads. Drop your old habits, change up your diet, alter your buying habits. Throw away your old self. If you're a smoker, stop. If you don't smoke, start. If you enjoy meat and hot and spicy foods, stop purchasing those items and change to vegan. If you frequent bars, stop. Patterns are predictable. Break them.

"When you get the chance, clip someone's wallet that looks like you. Don't kill them, or take the identity of someone who's already dead. GHOST Protocol looks for those algorithms in their complex computer programs. If someone is murdered and years later their information hits the system again applying for a job or renting an apartment, maybe take out a mortgage, they flag the name. And never get too comfortable in one place for too long. No small towns, you'll stand out too much and the people are too nosey and ask too many questions."

Cristal was grateful for his help. She found herself standing at the front door and hesitant to leave his place.

The Bishop stood closely by her and looked in her eyes. "You're smart, and you're a strong girl. Leave tonight. Don't come back."

She knew once she walked out that door she would never see him again. Cristal and The Bishop weren't ones to get emotional, but their look at each other said it all. There was a bizarre love and understanding between them.

He handed Cristal his car keys to the Wrangler.

"Thank you," she said.

"Just stay alive," were his last words to her.

She turned around and left. No looking back.

THIRTY-TWO

* *

Sharon stood in her black dress a few feet from the open grave close to the lane that ran the length of the cemetery. The dark brown casket, covered with flowers and wreaths, was ready to be lowered into the ground. The preacher stood by the casket, Bible in hand, clad in a black suit, and presided over the burial.

"When God saw you getting tired, and your life becoming fatigued, He reached out to you and placed His arms around you, and He said come to Me," the preacher said.

About thirty people showed up for Tamar's closed-casket funeral. Sharon hardly recognized any of them. She was mostly familiar with Tamar's siblings. Jada, Jason, and Lena were crying their eyes out, grieving over the loss of their sister. Black Earth didn't come to her own daughter's funeral.

Sharon stood there for a moment, under the gloomy clouds.

Soon, it began sprinkling. Little droplets of water came down during the service and began growing larger and falling more frequently. Raindrops dripped on Sharon as she stood frozen with her gaze fixed on the casket, saddened by the loss of Tamar. Though they hadn't been friends in years, it was still a tragedy to lose someone she grew up with.

She'd heard about the shooting on the ferry on the news. The media dubbed it "Woman Killed By Stray Bullet From Off-shore."

As the rain came crashing down and people put up their umbrellas, Sharon turned and walked away. She didn't want to stay for the end and see her friend lowered into the ground.

Walking toward her car, in the distance, she saw a figure that caught her attention. The person seemed transfixed from afar by Tamar's burial. From what Sharon could make out, it was a woman dressed in ordinary clothing and standing in the rain like it didn't bother her at all.

Cristal? Sharon questioned herself.

It had to be her.

Suddenly Sharon went running her way, calling out, "Cristal?"

The woman standing in the distance turned at hearing the name, gazed briefly at Sharon and steadily walked away. She disappeared down a small grade. When Sharon made it to where she saw the woman standing, it seemed like she had vanished into thin air. She stood there looking dumbfounded, her head swiveling in every direction.

The downpour made it harder to see. If it was Cristal, she made it clear that she didn't want to be seen.

Sharon felt like she was alone, all her friends dead and gone. She wasn't about to give up on finding Cristal, though. Whatever her friends were into, it had gotten them killed and had Cristal running for her life.

"I know you're alive and I know you're out there," Sharon exclaimed while standing in the heavy rain. "I'm still a friend, Cristal. I am. I miss you. Come home!"

She hurried to her car with a gut feeling she would never see her friend again.

THIRTY-THREE

* *

So many people were dead because of her. Her whole family had been wiped out, all her friends—Mona, Lisa, Tamar, Pike—dead. It wouldn't be long until they came after The Bishop for allowing her to live.

Why didn't he just do it? Cristal asked herself.

She hurried back to her Boston apartment and either destroyed everything or cleared it out. She packed money, guns, and essentials tightly into a duffel bag.

She had met with The Bishop's connect, the one he said she could trust, and for ten thousand dollars, she received a new passport, a social security card, and a new identity. Her new name was Jennifer Harris. It was basic, and didn't stand out. Jennifer meant "white enchantress" or "the fair one." Though her life was far from fair and she was no white enchantress, it would do for now.

Everything she was, she wasn't anymore, and with the Commission and GHOST Protocol gunning for her, she knew it would be only a matter of time before they found her. She couldn't afford any mistakes. And she couldn't risk going back to Boston, New York, or North Carolina.

She thought about Daniel a lot. She was going to miss him so much. It was going to break his heart when she didn't return. She was saving his life too. He would have to go on with his life, become a brain surgeon. He would be better off without her.

Thinking about him, a few tears trickled from her eyes. As she continued cleaning up her past, she sat down by her laptop and opened it up to the chapters to her fourth book, a few dozen pages.

"No more stories," she remembered The Bishop saying to her.

It was going to be hard. Writing was therapeutic for her. It was her way of getting back at everyone and destroying the Commission. But she would no longer be able to publish her writing. She would have to give it up, maybe write into a journal, but no more computers. No more writing under a pseudonym. Melissa Chin was finally dead.

It was hard for her, but she pressed the delete button and eliminated everything she had written for her fourth book. Cristal let out a deep sigh and picked up her laptop with both hands, lifted it over her head, and smashed it against the desk repeatedly. Pieces went flying everywhere. It was a hard thing to do, but it had to be done.

The apartment, everything had been wiped down clean, thrown away, or destroyed. There was nothing left to remind anyone that she ever lived there. No pictures, no trinkets or any clothing of her, all burned or tossed into the trash.

The only thing she had left was memories.

Cristal didn't know where she was going. She had no family, and even if she did, she couldn't run to them and compromise their safety too.

She walked out her apartment door for the final time, with no intention of coming back. She had the keys to The Bishop's Wrangler, but she couldn't take advantage of the Jeep for too long. It would be like leaving bread crumbs behind.

She took off in it, heading west on I-90, and then when she reached Jamestown, a small town in upstate New York, she sold the Jeep for cash and hopped on the Greyhound bus toward Seattle, Washington.

Lots of rain and bad weather. Lots of people staying indoors.

THIRTY-FOUR

A swarm of assassins clad in black and carrying high-powered rifles quickly descended on the cottage in the middle of the night. First, they took out the lights and then rushed toward the place carefully. They were fully aware of The Bishop's frightful résumé. He was one of the best assassins in the country, so the team of killers couldn't take any chances. They came in heavy and ready, fully expecting that The Bishop wouldn't go down easily.

The killers in black, looking like trained Navy SEALs, carefully crouched low near the cottage, camouflaged by the night and thick shrubberies, their guns gripped and their attention on every detail of the dark, still cottage, the doors closed, the windows black, and his vehicle gone.

But it all could be deception. The Bishop was known to set booby traps, or catch an individual off guard, and they would soon find a knife thrust into their windpipe or spine. He was a crack shot from any distance, and when it came to hand-to-hand combat, the man was nothing to play with. He had been known to take out a group of men with lightning speed, breaking necks and snapping limbs apart.

The four assassins working for GHOST Protocol moved forward with caution, assuming The Bishop was gearing up for war.

"We wait for the signal," the leader said.

Each one nodded.

•••

Inside the cottage, The Bishop sat on his small stool in front of his white canvas on the easel. He was bringing to life his own portrait—his stark white hair, matching goatee, and his muscular build. In the portrait he was wearing a blue suit. He painted himself in a tranquil place, a colorful garden filled with flowers and trees. It was his personal paradise.

The music playing in the background this time was *Les Misérables*, the French musical. It was his favorite, set in early nineteenth-century France, telling the story of a French peasant named Jean Valjean and his quest for redemption after serving nineteen years in jail for stealing a loaf of bread for his sister's starving child.

The Bishop listened to the story being told and appreciated the quality of the orchestra and singers playing through his speakers.

He was dressed in a suit as he painted. He looked sharp and handsome in a dark gray suit, dark blue tie, and alligator shoes. He was dressed to kill, for a night out on the town. He held the paintbrush with finesse, bringing the multicolored garden alive with every stroke against the canvas. He remained focused and determined to complete it.

He was aware of the killers lingering outside the cottage, yet he kept cool and unperturbed, as if he was the only one there, as if waiting for a date to show up. The painting kept his mind occupied. It was turning out to be his finest masterpiece.

He smiled at it.

He heard a slight disturbance near the window. They were coming for him soon. He still had the skills to take out as many operatives as were swarming his property. He could have easily plucked them away one by one, given them all a rude awakening. Yet he continued to sit and paint.

The Bishop was no longer the man he used to be—a coldblooded killer who could shoot the wings off a fly. He was done with murders. He was done with this life. He was enjoying his retirement. He was taking pleasure with his pastime.

They were waiting for something. He knew it.

A few moments went by, and his artwork was finally finished. It looked like it belonged in an art museum—the Smithsonian or the Metropolitan. What he had finished painting was priceless. It was his legacy.

He felt a presence behind him. He didn't turn to face it, but continued gazing at his painting.

"It's beautiful," the voice behind him said.

"Thank you," The Bishop returned, looking impassive.

The Glock 17 with the suppressor at the end was raised to the back of his head. He never turned around to face his killer. He simply kept gazing at his painting, it being the last thing he wanted to see.

Poot! Poot! Poot!

Three shots slammed into the back of The Bishop's skull, and he collapsed face down in front of his artwork.

His killer walked toward the body and gazed down at him, expressionless. She was in all black, a long ponytail dangling from the back of her head, the smoking gun still in her hand. It would become a piece of history, the weapon that took out a heartless and skilled killer. The assassin who held it was very familiar with the man she had just killed.

"You should have killed that bitch," she whispered. "I will always love you."

It was Natalia, his girlfriend. She was a secret agent assigned to look after and keep tabs on The Bishop. When he failed to kill Cristal, Natalia made the phone call to her superiors, and they gave her the contract. She wouldn't make the same mistakes he made. She loved him, but her life and career came first.

Natalia pivoted on her shoes and walked away from the body. Murdergram fulfilled.

THIRTY-FIVE

●●●

Daniel was excited. Beatrice was supposed to be returning home to him from Africa. He missed her more than ever. It had been five weeks since he had last seen her, and he couldn't wait to wrap his arms around his lovely woman and hold her forever. Not hearing from her, their only communication letters via snail mail, was a struggle. The wait was no more. Today was the day.

He ran around his small shotgun home cleaning up. He washed dishes, swept every inch of the house, did laundry, and spruced the place up a little by painting the walls. He placed a bouquet of store-bought flowers in a homemade coffee-can vase and cooked a meal of catfish, rice and peas, and cornbread for her. She would be hungry returning from her long trip.

It was almost 7 p.m., and her bus would arrive in less than a half hour. In the last letter he had received from Beatrice, she informed him that she would be home a week before the Christmas holidays.

Daniel took one last look at his place, and everything looked orderly. He wasn't exactly a neat freak, which drove

Beatrice crazy, but he'd managed to do his best. He knew she would be happy with how it turned out.

He hurried out the door and jumped into his Civic. The ride to Charlotte wasn't far, but he didn't want to be late. He wanted to be right there when her bus pulled into the station.

Daniel arrived in time to see the bus Beatrice was scheduled to be pull in, but she wasn't on it. *Maybe she missed it,* he thought.

The next bus came and still no Beatrice.

Two hours went by.

He started to worry. He attempted to call her cell phone numerous times, but it kept going to voicemail. By the fourth hour of waiting at the bus station, he was almost into a full-blown panic. It was time to notify the police.

The officer advised him that they couldn't file a missing-person report on his girlfriend until twenty-four hours had passed. Daniel became frantic. He tried not to think the worst, but he couldn't help it.

"Where is she!" he exclaimed, wandering about nervously.

He knew something was wrong. He could feel it. Beatrice would never have stood him up like this. She was always punctual with her arrival.

When he climbed into his car, he couldn't control the tears trickling down his face. He couldn't go anywhere at the moment. He felt paralyzed with worry. Something was definitely wrong. He could feel it.

...

Cristal knew it had to be done. Walking away from Daniel was a hard choice, one of the hardest she had to make. She had wrestled with her options. She could either walk away and never look back, or snatch him up, tell him the truth about who she really was, and hope that he'd forgive her and give up his life as he knew it to live out his years with her on the run.

But she just couldn't be that selfish. To save his life, she had to leave. She had chosen the life she was in. If she had to do it all over again, she would have never walked into that white church with the steeple. At the time she didn't think she had options. She was young and naïve, and her future seemed bleak.

After meeting Daniel and falling in love with him, Cristal realized that all she had to do was work hard, stay focused, and she could have made any dream she had come true.

She was an hour away from Seattle two transfers later. The trip was a smooth one. She sat alone in the seat, peering out the window. On both sides of the highway an immense wasteland stretched for miles into the horizon. Everything looked desolate and stagnant. The bus roared up the highway. It was the only sound for miles around.

As the bus pulled into the Seattle, she felt a little relief mixed with uncertainty. It was going to be her first time in the city.

Cristal stepped of the Greyhound clutching her duffel bag of guns and money, and instantly took notice of her surroundings. The bus station wasn't anything like New York's or Boston's; it was busy, but the crowd seemed to be fading fast, whereas in the bigger cities, the people coming and going seemed perpetual.

With her new identity and enough money to last, Cristal wondered how long this would be her home. Seattle had a magnificent setting, with the snowy peak of Mount Rainier in the distance, a modern skyline of glass skyscrapers, a friendly charm, and plenty of fun coffeehouses, good restaurants, and engaging clubs.

She planned on staying away from it all.

THIRTY-SIX

. . . .

The cell phone ringing in the next room startled Daniel from his brief sleep. It was four in the morning. Trying to retrieve his phone, he jumped out of bed, collided with the coffee table, and banged his knee. "Ahh!"

He had been up most of the night drinking Red Bull and black coffee, hoping Beatrice would walk through the door any minute.

"Hello!" he spat into the phone, eager to hear her voice.

"Can I speak to a Daniel?"

"Speaking," he immediately announced.

"You don't know me, but I'm Beatrice's aunt."

"Is she okay? Where is she?" Daniel nervously asked.

For a moment, there was silence from the other end. The silence made Daniel even more nervous.

"I'm afraid I have some bad news," the aunt said gently.

Daniel took a seat on the couch, bracing himself for the bad news.

"I received a call from the Red Cross. They sadly informed me that Beatrice was killed in Uganda during a revolt by the villagers."

"No! No! No!" he hollered, falling to his knees as his eyes immediately began to water up. "Please, no!"

The aunt continued with, "I'm sorry. Her body is going to be cremated, and unfortunately there won't be a memorial because of financial constraints."

Daniel continued to sob. He had fallen to the floor. He couldn't believe it. *She is dead!*

"I'm sorry," the fake aunt said.

He didn't have much to say himself. The only thing he could ask for was her remains, and she promised to send it all to him. Daniel remained against the floor for hours sobbing. It was hard to believe she was gone.

EPILOGUE

●●●●●●●●●●●●●●●●●●●●●●●●●●●●●●●●●●●●●

EIGHTEEN MONTHS LATER

Hundreds of people gathered in the large open area at Johnson C. Smith University in Charlotte, North Carolina for the graduation ceremony on a beautiful May day. A crowd of seniors in their blue caps and long blue gowns flooded the grassy area. They were all smiling, laughing, and congratulating each other. They had come a long way, four years or more of midterms and late study nights. Now, they were ready to march across the stage and receive their diplomas and degrees.

Spring was now well advanced and had sprinkled the meadows with lovely flowers, and the trees were coming alive with greenery. The sunlight flooded the many graduates and their family seated in their chairs. There was a sea of matching blue in the front rows, the graduates seated silently and listening to the dean's speech about growth and prosperity.

Daniel was among the graduates ready to march across the stage to receive his degree in his medical field. In fact, he was named the class's valedictorian. He'd studied hard and long, and he was inching his way closer to becoming a brain surgeon. He had been accepted and given a full scholarship to Johns Hopkins University and would start in the fall

He sat in the front row, holding onto an urn and feeling proud of everything he had accomplished. But he still felt a little empty without Beatrice in his life. In the urn he carried her ashes, supposedly. Wherever he went, he kept the urn close to him.

As the dean wrapped up his "Prosperity" speech to the graduates in front of him, Daniel was little nervous about going up to give his own speech to the class. He took a deep breath and clutched the urn tightly.

"And now," the dean announced. "I would like to call up the university's valedictorian, Daniel Roberts."

Daniel stood up and gripped the urn. He headed toward the stage and stood behind the podium ready to deliver his valedictorian commencement speech. He gazed into the attentive crowd of faces, placed the urn on the podium, cleared his throat, and started his speech.

●●●

Unbeknownst to him, deep in the crowd watching and smiling was Cristal. She was in profound disguise, keeping alert of everything around her. It was a risk coming back, but she wouldn't miss this day even if it was going to cost her her life. She assumed there would be numerous assassins looking for her, so she came ready with a concealed pistol.

She watched Daniel standing at the podium, looking handsome and educated, and she was so proud of him. She wished she could hug and kiss him, experience his happiness with him, but it wasn't happening. The only thing she could do was observe him from afar and be happy for him.

She sat and listened to him speak.

He started with, "One of the most unbelievably courageous people I've met once told me that tomorrow isn't promised to anyone, so how can you plan for it? Well, I can tell you how."

Cristal listened intently and beamed with pride as she listened to his speech that was filled with hope, nostalgia, and sheer optimism.

As the crowd began to disperse, she spotted two notable assassins scouring the crowd. She was sure there were more. If today was her last day on earth, seeing Daniel in his element made it all worth it.

Don't Let the Dollface Fool You

 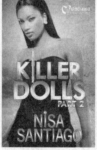 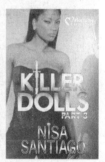

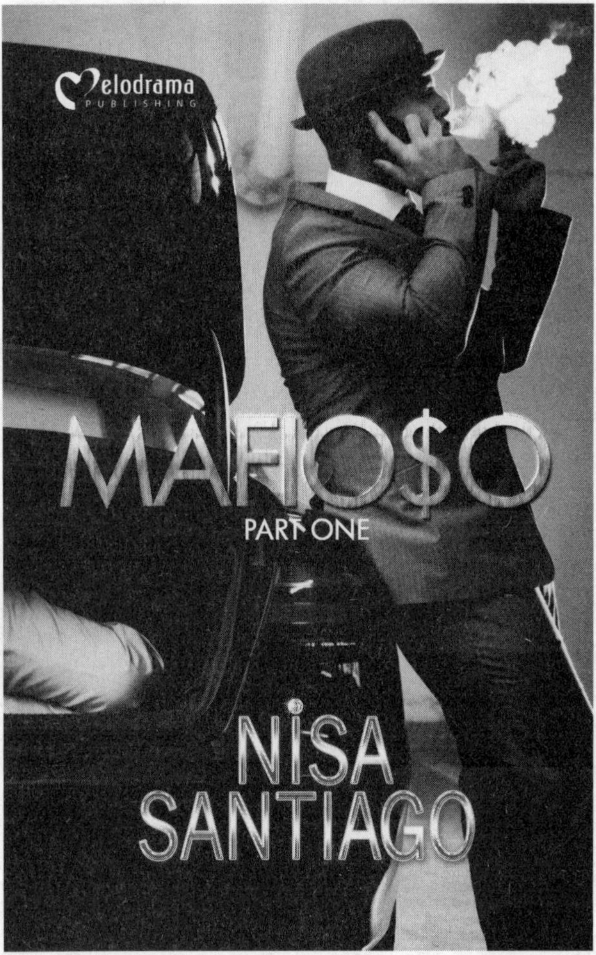
Melodrama
PUBLISHING
MAFIO$O
PART ONE
NISA
SANTIAGO

FOLLOW
NISA SANTIAGO

FACEBOOK.COM/NISASANTIAGO

INSTAGRAM.COM/NISA_SANTIAGO

TWITTER.COM/NISA_SANTIAGO